A LAND OF
PURE DELIGHT

A LAND OF PURE DELIGHT

Elijah Morgan & the Saints of Bethel

A witty, erudite and affectionate evocation of
Welsh rural life in the 1950s

ISAAC OWEN

RESOURCE *Publications* · Eugene, Oregon

A LAND OF PURE DELIGHT
Elijah Morgan and the Saints of Bethel

Resource publications
A Division of Wipf and Stock Publishers
199 W. 8th Ave., Suite 3
Eugene, OR 97401

www.wipfandstock.com

ISBN 13: 978-1-62032-407-3

Manufactured in the U.S.A.

Contents

1

Mr Elijah Morgan
is Called to Bethel

Far from the grime of coalfields, the clangour of steelworks, the bustle of slate quarries there lies, in remotest Wales, a secluded valley. It is criss-crossed by narrow roads, many of them without signposts. This causes little trouble because most of the families in the valley have been there for generations. The focal point of the valley for shopping and gossip is the village: one general store, one pub, two petrol pumps, a Norman church and about 150 residents. But the centre of the religious and social life of the valley is to be found a mile outside the village, just half a mile from the sea. It is Bethel Congregational Chapel.

The chapel stands on a small rise surrounded by its graveyard. Beyond that, on two sides are fields inhabited now by sheep, now by cattle. On the third side is the Manse, standing in its large garden. Opposite, across the minor road which leads to the village and the sea in one direction, and to town in the other, are two cottages and an area of deciduous woodland, home to a variety of birds and small animals, and a beautiful sight at bluebell-time.

On the last Sunday in April 1953 Mr Elijah Morgan from the Theological College came to preach at Bethel with a view to the pastor-ate. In the final year of his studies, and with a BA already under his belt, he was highly recommended by the College Principal, Dr Morgan MacDonald. The Principal's role in times of pastoral vacancy was always of a somewhat episcopal kind – though, of course, Congregationalists do not have bishops.

Elijah came from the other side of Wales, and this was his first visit to the county, never mind to Bethel. He travelled on the Saturday because

1

the journey was long: a bus from College to the station; two trains with an hour-long wait between them; and finally the seven-mile journey from Newbridge to Bethel on the local bus run by the Edwards Brothers. The bus had seen better days. It was in good mechanical order because Bob Edwards spent an hour or so each evening lying under it or peering into its engine while his brother Alf totted up the day's takings. But in terms of decor it left something to be desired. It was painted brown and yellow, and the offside was dented following a mishap with a hay wagon. As passengers boarded they were greeted by an official notice bearing the command, 'Do not spit on the bus'. Two wartime posters still adorned the glass panel behind the driver. Of these the first proclaimed that 'Coughs and sneezes spread diseases. Trap the germs in your handkerchief.' – 'A sensible enough injunction in peacetime too', thought Elijah as a passenger behind him had a sneezing fit without benefit of handkerchief. The other poster assured travellers, 'We are trying to get you a wider seat.' 'No luck yet, then,' Elijah mused and, indeed, the poster proclaimed a falsehood. Far from exerting themselves to obtain wider seats, the brothers were perfectly happy with the wooden slatted ones already in place. They were economical and practical. Drunken youths returning home from town on a Saturday night could not slash them – though they could carve their initials on them with their pen knives, and some did; while a quick scrub down between stops was no problem if, as a special favour, or in consideration of a dozen eggs or some home brew, a few hens, a sheep or a pig had been permitted to join the human passengers.

As compared with the first three conveyances he had been on that day, the bus was a moving village. Most of the passengers knew one another well. They exchanged news. They ran down those who would be on the next bus. What they did not do was to admire the scenery, which was beautiful, but which had been their environment since they first took breath. Some of them took a proprietary interest in particular seats, and woe betide any 'foreigner' who inadvertently failed to intuit this fact. The locals would huff and puff, and generally make it clear to any interloper that this was how international disputes over territorial rights started.

Elijah, of course, knew none of them, and he supposed that nobody knew him. How wrong he was. He had not reckoned with that mixture of gossip and amateur skills of detection by which the folk of Bethel charted their course. Who else would be in his Sunday suit on a Saturday afternoon, carrying a suitcase and travelling to Bethel but the theological student 'on appro.'? Elijah, who was sitting in the front seat, had the creepy feeling that he was being closely observed from behind – as indeed he was. And he was quite sure that the occupants of the bus did not generally converse in whispers. One passenger was either not a skilled whisperer, or the recipient of his comment was hard of hearing; for Elijah distinctly heard the words, 'He'll never go to Bethel. He's got a BA. He's far too good for you lot.' 'Not a Bethel member,' concluded Elijah; 'probably the village atheist.'

At Bethel chapel, there was a bus stop – the last before the terminus in the village – and Elijah knew he had to alight there. As he made for the door he wickedly wondered whether he should turn and bless all the passengers with the sign of the cross – just to tease and confuse them. But you never knew where the deacons were, so he thanked the driver, got off, and had his first sight of Bethel chapel.

Of plain design and inexpensive construction, the front wall of Bethel had a central door with windows on either side that, in certain lights, look like elongated eyes peering out onto a sinful world. Set in the wall above the door was a simple plaque, host to several forms of biological life, and inscribed thus:

> Founded 1676 – First Chapel Erected 1702 – Second chapel erected 1830, enlarged 1906.

The dates were significant. It is said that the cause originated in the labours of two itinerant ministers who were ejected from their Anglican livings following the Act of Uniformity of 1662. They and about two thousand others could not agree that the monarch or parliament had the right to say how the Church should worship and be governed. 'Christ alone', they said, 'is Lord of the Church.'

Although Elijah had never seen Bethel before he felt that he knew quite a lot about it. Church History was among his favourite subjects, and he had been delighted when Geraint Pritchard, the Professor of that subject, had called him to his room a few days before. Professor Pritchard really looked the part. The faintly musty aroma of old books and archives had seeped into his well-worn clothes. Slightly built, of angular features and a languid manner, there was a desiccated look about him, except for a luxuriant long beard which seemed to suck all the vitality from the rest of his body. If students wanted to divert him from his lecture notes they had only to ask, 'Do you think Isaac Watts was really a Unitarian by the time he died?' This question always touched Pritchard on the raw – that anyone should think that his hero – a pioneer hymn writer, philosopher and theologian – was a Unitarian!! But he knew that his opposite number at the Unitarian College thought exactly that, and he was hard put to resist the conclusion that that infidel had written an article on the subject just to spite him. With Unitarians to the left of him and Wesleyans to the right, the latter falsely claiming that all was religiously dark in the eighteenth century until John Wesley clip-clopped into view, Professor Pritchard had his polemical work cut out. More than once he had felt like David among the Philistines and Ammonites.

Pritchard was soaked in the Congregational tradition. In one respect only did he flout the general convention among Welsh Congregationalists. He wore a clerical collar on Sundays. However this was completely hidden by his beard, and he could have worn a spiv's kipper tie and got away with it.

'Come in, dear boy,' he said as Elijah knocked on his door. 'I hear you are to preach with a view to the pastorate at Bethel?'

'Yes,' said Elijah, whereupon the learned Professor became enraptured with historical detail and enveloped in reverent piety.

'Ah! the saints of yore,' he began, 'what they suffered for those liberties which we take too often for granted! Freedom of worship – a precious pearl! Liberty of conscience – a right they died for! Who will you stay with?' he asked, apparently coming down to earth.

'With Mr and Mrs Jenkin Jones of Top Farm,' Elijah replied – and Pritchard was off again:

'Top Farm! A haven of godly praise in an impious land! For there, my boy, in that very farmhouse did the ejected ministers lead their clandestine flock in the days of persecution. They lived dangerously, meeting in barns and caves and homes. What pains they suffered! What indignities they endured! Do make sure that Farmer Jones shows you where the escape door was in his dining room.'

'Escape door?' queried Elijah.

'Yes. Their meetings for worship took place in his dining room. There was a small pulpit at one end, and behind it a door, so that the preacher could escape if any informants had alerted the officers of the law to their illegal worship. If you go there you will enter into a goodly heritage.'

Elijah was about to ask a question when the Professor hurtled out of his chair with a degree of agility of which Elijah had hitherto thought him quite incapable. He was like a fox after a rabbit. He shot over to the other side of the room where there was a locked bookcase. He took a key from his pocket and opened the cupboard. 'Here', he declared, 'is my treasure chest.'

Elijah could see at a glance that nothing of immediate pecuniary value was in the cupboard. But he could also see that it contained old books neatly arranged. Pritchard went straight to the one he wanted.

'See,' he said triumphantly, 'this is the Church Book of Bethel!'

He brought it over to Elijah and reverently opened it. 'This book tells the history of the church in the words and handwriting of its literate members,' he said. 'On the first page we have the covenant written in 1676 and signed by the first members.'

Elijah's excitement mounted. He looked at the covenant which began, 'We poor worms, lost in Adam, who have received salvation through Christ, solemnly covenant with one another to walk before God in all his ways and to worship him only.' It went on to outline their principal beliefs, and it declared their intention to be a body 'disciplined under the Lord'. Fifteen members had signed the covenant or put their cross to it – eight of them Joneses.

'Turn over,' said Professor Pritchard. Elijah did so, and on the next page he found an account of the rejoicing of the members when the Toleration Act of 1689 gave them freedom of worship. They expressed their determination to build a chapel to the glory of God and, as the tablet on the present chapel indicated, this they achieved in 1702. A description of the chapel was given. It was a plain, rectangular building with a three-decker pulpit on the long wall, facing a gallery on the opposite wall. The building was financed largely by farm labourers and a few fishermen, and its foundations were never secure. It became dangerous – a circumstance sombrely recorded in the Church Book and, in 1830, it was replaced. This second building was enlarged in 1906, in the wake of the Revival of 1904 when, according to folk memory, a huge number of the perishing were rescued: drunkards, burglars, wife-beaters and assorted atheists, secularists and pagans of one kind or another, were converted. They came piling into Bethel and the accommodation problem became acute – especially since some of the new converts, possessed by the Spirit, took to dancing in the aisle and even collapsing in convulsing heaps in front of the Lord's table. So the pulpit wall was pushed back, and more room was made. Sometimes visiting Congregationalists viewed Bethel askance. *Their* chapel had been designed by the prince of chapel architects, Thomas Thomas, and was in the Gothic style with traceried flowing Decorated windows. But Thomas was but thirteen in 1830, and had been dead for eighteen years in 1906, so on neither occasion was he in a position to advise the saints at Bethel.

It was clear from the Church Book that at the regular Church Meeting which all members were expected to attend, 'discipline under the Lord' was taken very seriously. Elijah thought that some of the members seemed to enjoy discipline a little too much. Brother Davies was reprimanded for arriving at church in a drunken state; Sister Francis was banned from communion for six months for being unwed and with child; and so it went on. And all of this was presided over by the minister whose loyal, and sometimes less than fully loyal, henchmen were the deacons elected by the Church Meeting to share in the spiritual and material leadership of the flock.

All of this was in Elijah's mind as he stood looking at Bethel chapel. He could not wait to see what it was like inside. That would be a treat for tomorrow. Now he must make his way to Top Farm, two hundred yards up the hill. On the way he passed a field with sheep in it, and then came to another in which was a herd of Jersey cows. There were barns to the right. He could see hay in one of them, he heard a horse neigh in another, and in a third he saw a tractor. Then came the house. A delightful old farmhouse with 1630 carved in the stonework over the front porch.

Elijah rang the bell.

'Come in,' called out a voice, 'we don't stand on ceremony here.'

'They don't lock their doors either,' thought Elijah, having lived in town during six years of College.

The voice was that of Dilys Jones. Elijah stepped into the hall, and as he did so she appeared in her best apron. She was a cheerful soul of ample proportions, who would never accept a guest's attempt to refuse second helpings of her equally ample cuisine.

'We've been looking forward to your visit,' she said, 'and I hope you'll feel at home here.'

Elijah, thinking that he could see no reason why he should not feel at home, said that he, too, was pleased to be there and honoured to be invited to preach at Bethel.

'Come through to the kitchen,' said Dilys. Elijah followed her into a huge room. At one end hams were hanging from the rafters on large hooks. On the wall opposite the window was an enormous Welsh dresser on which were displayed numerous souvenir plates, many of them depicting chapels. At one end was a sturdy oak table.

'Sit down,' she said, and he did so. In a flash a plate of Welsh cakes appeared, followed by cheese and biscuits and an enormous pot of tea. 'Tuck in,' said Dilys, 'but be sure to leave room for the meal.' Elijah had thought that this was the meal, and only with difficulty did he leave room for later: the food was so tempting.

As he was eating Dilys went to the back door and yelled, 'Jenkin! He's here!' And within a minute or two Elijah heard someone scraping his boots at the scullery door, and in came Mr Jenkin Jones in his socks. He was a wiry man with a weather-beaten face. His bald pate protruded above a residue of iron grey curls. He was an aromatic presence, with pipe tobacco lingering on his clothes, and (except when in his socks) more local odours wafting upwards from his boots. Jenkin was the senior deacon and church secretary. He had been church secretary for thirty-five years. During forty years as secretary his father had served (or seen off) three ministers before Mr Rees arrived. Jenkin had only known the late Reverend Goronwy Rees. Jenkin was a kind man, but a man of few words, except when pleading before the Lord in prayer.

'I'm glad to meet you,' he said. 'How was your journey?' And so for the next half hour they got to know one another. Then Jenkin said, 'I must now go off to do the milking. Have a look at *The Farmer's Weekly* while I'm gone.'

The thought that anyone would not find the contents of that worthy paper utterly riveting had never crossed Jenkin's mind. At all events, Elijah got himself up to date with stock prices, the latest machinery, and all the other matters with which dedicated farmers filled their minds. The milking done, they all sat down to a superb meal of soup, roast beef, and bread and butter pudding. To Elijah it was like manna in the wilderness – though it was more substantial than manna, and Top Farm was by no means a wilderness. But, as theological students the land over knew, weekend preaching appointments afforded the one occasion in the week to eat their fill, for College meals either did not fill, or could hardly be eaten. After this sumptuous meal there was more conversation; the place where the escape door for preachers disturbed by the officers of the law, its outline clearly visible through the plastered wall, was proudly pointed out; and then bed. It was a feather bed and after almost a term of avoiding a protruding spring in the mattress of his College bed, it was, to Elijah, as if he were having a foretaste of eternal bliss.

He slept well, and after an enormous breakfast they all set off for the morning service. Elijah had his first glimpse inside Bethel. Inside the front door was a small vestibule. In it was a table on which were neatly stacked copies of *The Congregational Hymnary*, the saints of Bethel not as yet having got their minds or their finances around to the recently published *Congregational Praise*. The pulpit was opposite the front door; the communion table, given in memory of the late, greatly revered minister, the Reverend Goronwy Rees, was in front of it.

The American organ was to the left. The organ had seen better days. It sounded asthmatical at certain times of the year. Mrs Blodwen Llewellyn, LRAM, was the organist. The faster she peddled, the more the air escaped. Her face reddened – never more so than after the sixth verse of 'The first Nowell'. If ever Butlins exchanged knobbly knees competitions for muscular calf competitions, Blodwen would win hands down. By the side of the organ was a small music cabinet in which Blodwen kept her vast store of voluntaries for the American organ and harmonium. She had all twelve volumes of Caleb Simper's voluntaries, *The Cathedral Voluntaries* by Frank L. Moir and Carl Bergman, and a number of those arranged by J. W. Elliott. Designed to foster an atmosphere of worship, they actually seemed to legitimate conversations in the pews which fluctuated in volume according to dynamics of the music. It is no adverse criticism of Blodwen to say that some members of the congregation noticed the music only when it stopped. Sometimes Blodwen would catch the congregation out by rising through a crescendo to fortissimo, and then suddenly stopping, leaving them all shouting at one another. When they realised that there was no music, they would look a little shamefaced and subside into a variety of attitudes of preparatory prayer.

To the right of the pulpit a door led into the Sunday School room. It had a tiny scullery attached, a platform at one end, and a seating capacity of about eighty. To the left of the pulpit was a door leading to a vestry, the walls of which were crammed with likenesses of former ministers, some of whom looked so stern that it was as if they were defying any successor to enter the room after they were gone. The schoolroom and vestry were part of the 1906 extensions. The toilet, one of the more temperamental of its class, was outside, and was generally frequented in extremity only by human beings, and by hibernating hedgehogs in the winter months.

Mr Morgan faced the challenge by which so many Welsh ministers are faced. As he walked into Bethel on the Sunday morning, Blodwen Llewellyn accosted him, thrust an old brown envelope into his hand on which were scrawled four numbers and said, 'Here is the order of service'. Elijah gathered that these were hymn numbers – though they might equally well have been Blodwen's husband's tax return destined for his accountant; indeed, on one occasion, so it was said, they were.

Everyone had turned out. Those who never attended morning service because of the Sunday roast made do with a salad. Those who could never come out at night because of the milking made alternative arrangements with and for their beasts. The chapel was full for both services.

Into the pulpit stepped Mr Morgan. He was of medium build, had a slightly puckish expression, and had fair, wavy hair. But it was his eyes which really caught the attention of the mothers who had daughters in their early twenties: blue, bright, intelligent, and with a look which suggested that only after a struggle had sanctity overcome mischief. Mrs Mavis Long thought, 'He'd be lovely for my Angela', and two rows behind Mrs Gloria Phillips began to envisage a match between Mr Morgan and her Valerie. Quite oblivious to all such scheming thoughts, Elijah began the service. Between Blodwen's four numbers Elijah sandwiched his prayers, Bible readings and sermon. He did the same in the evening with four different numbers, different readings , prayers and sermon, and both services seemed to go quite well.

Between the two services Elijah was entertained by David and Betty Pugh. Mr Pugh was a deacon and church treasurer. It was commitment to this latter vocation that prompted him to insist on giving hospitality to the visiting student. He thought it important to see how expensive his tastes might be when it came to redecorating the Manse and suchlike. Anyone who saw Mr Pugh on a weekday would be under no misapprehension that he worked outdoors. He was, in fact, a skilled gardener. His ruddy complexion, tousled hair, wiry strength, string-tied corduroys and hobnailed boots marked him out at once as a son of the soil. On Sundays, apart from his ruddy complexion, he looked strangely transformed – and uncomfortable. He was very proud of the fact that he could still (just) get into his wedding suit, waistcoat and all. The gold chain of his pocket watch drifted across his stomach, and his shirt was as white as snow, and as stiff as a board, for Betty was very liberal with the starch. If was as if she regarded starch as the modern equivalent of flagellation, an inducement to deep spirituality. When somebody informed Mr Pugh that the founder of the Reckitt's starch company was from a Quaker family he was appalled that a person from such a gentle, pacific, tradition should have entertained such a cruel way of making money – a Methodist, perhaps. Mr Pugh was so staunch a Congregationalist that he would allow no cigarettes to stain his remaining teeth but Gold Flake, because Gold Flake came from W. H. and D. O. Wills, the Congregational benefactors of Bristol. That fact, of course, did nothing to eradicate Mr Pugh's occasional 'nasty cough.'

Mr Pugh had been appointed treasurer some years before, when it was discovered that as a youth he had taken a book-keeping course at night school and (which commended him even more highly to the Bethel deacons) that he had a profound mistrust of banks. Hence his nickname, by which he will be hereinafter known, Dai Cashbox. The box in question had never been seen by any person other than Dai, who kept it under his bed. Never was a church treasurer more consistent in his annual reporting to the Church Meeting. When called upon to present his findings Dai invariably affirmed with great confidence, 'All's OK', whereupon he received the thanks of the church for his faithful service.

The Pughs' son, Adrian, was sixteen. Like his father, he loved the outdoor life, and after lunch he volunteered to take Elijah for a stroll to give him the lie of the land. The interval between Sunday services was always a hazardous time for theological students. There was no end to the things their hosts might invite them to do. Some would sheepishly say, 'Would you like to read the paper?' – the buying of papers on the Lord's Day being frowned upon in some circles. Others would contrive to marry off their daughters; a few who owned cars would suggest a drive around the district; and too many would suggest a stroll. These strolls could become route marches, and theological students who had been undernourished all the week, and sitting up until midnight slaving over Hebrew grammar, were not in the best condition for such exploits.

'I'd love to go,' said Elijah, hoping for the best. So off he went with Adrian. The countryside around Bethel village was delightful: rolling hills, a stream, meadows, and, higher up, some rough common land. As might have been predicted, Adrian made straight for the rough common land. Up and up they went, and spongier and spongier became the land with its moss and scrubby vegetation – and Elijah in his Sunday best and with one service to go. Eventually they reached the summit and the view almost made Elijah's soiled shoes worthwhile. In the distance were the ruins of an old Welsh castle.

'When was that built?' asked Elijah.

'Ages ago,' said Adrian, not very informatively stating the obvious. Elijah tried once more:

'Was it ruined in battle with the English?'

'It was either that, or else the locals used the stone for their houses and barns.'

Elijah was too out of breath to pursue the matter any further, and in any case he had an evening service to get to. So they hurried back for tea. Betty Pugh gave Elijah the wherewithal to clean his shoes, at the same time scolding Adrian for taking the minister on such a gruelling and muddy walk; and they got to the chapel by the skin of their teeth.

After the service there was yet another huge meal back at Top Farm; another good night's sleep in the feather bed; an enormous breakfast on the Monday morning; and fond farewells. Elijah thanked the Joneses most warmly for their kindness and, as he left to walk to the bus stop, Dilys said, 'I hope we shall see you again.'

Just as the bus came into view there was a clattering of hobnails on the road, and up came Dai Cashbox, panting hard. He thrust an envelope into Elijah's hand. 'Here's your fee and expenses,' he puffed, 'nearly forgot; safe journey!' The bus door closed, and Elijah was away on the long journey home. He did not realise that he had just passed a supreme test. Dai Cashbox thought of little else but money, but he mightily approved of ministers who thought very little of it. The fact that the visitor had not mentioned Dai's carefully planned 'oversight' on the previous evening caused Elijah to shoot up in the treasurer's estimation. This, more than anything Elijah had said in his sermons, would weigh with Dai when the deacons met to consider the next step regarding Mr Morgan.

To all except the women of the catering committee, the deacons were the powers in the land. At 7.30 p.m. on the Monday evening the deacons forgathered. (The Bethel deacons did not do anything so common as 'meet', 'Deaconin'' being 'serious work' as Jenkin Jones once reminded one of the less-engaged brethren.) Their task was to pass judgement on Mr Morgan, and make a recommendation to the Church Meeting either that he be called to the pastorate, or not. In view of the importance of the occasion (and also because he could stand only so much excitement) Jenkin Jones the church secretary had invited the minister from town to conduct the meeting: 'So as to see fair play,' he explained, somewhat indelicately, to the other deacons.

The minister from Newbridge was a man whose reputation was as great as his sermons were incomprehensible: the Reverend Dr Iorwerth Lewis. He was every inch the scholar – and there were seventy-six inches of him. He was pale of countenance, as thin as a rake, slightly stooped, and with the largest Adam's apple you ever did see. Further indications of his scholarly nature were his thick glasses, and his suit which had seen better days. The trousers seemed always to be pulling away from the waistcoat as if the two had had a row, and this resulted in the sartorial condition known as 'concertina legs'. Dr Iorwerth Lewis was no common or garden PhD. He had earned the Doctorate of Divinity by publishing a massive study of Denys the Pseudo-Areopagite. This at once set him apart from all other Congregational ministers and, indeed, from most of the rest of the human race. So abstruse were his sermons that when, after one of them, Nellie said to Ethel, 'Wasn't he grand this morning?' and Ethel replied, 'You surely didn't understand him!' Nellie sighed, 'Of course not; but what a lovely sensation when those long words whistle past your lugs!' As for the practicalities of daily life, the mysticism of the Pseudo-Areopagite had all but taken him over. It was said that Iorwerth Lewis, DD, did not know that his two boys had been thieving until they were up before the court. Assuredly, nothing in his extensive studies had prepared him for the deacons at Bethel. Yet there they were around the table – five men and the formidable Mrs Rachel Morris.

Dr Lewis sat at the head of the table, flanked by Jenkin Jones and Dai Cashbox. Next to Dai sat Albert Williams. He was thick-set, and, like Dai Cashbox, was ruddy of hue, though for his complexion the sun and the outdoor life generally were in no way responsible. He was wearing a blazer bearing the badge of his wartime regiment, and on the table in front of him he carefully placed his beloved trilby. He was born in the village, but left when he volunteered for armed service in 1914. After the First World War he set up home in the Valleys, where work was more plentiful. He worked in the coal mines, and became something of a presence in the local branch of the Miners' Federation of Great Britain, which became the National Union of Mineworkers on 1 January 1945. On retirement three years before, he had returned to his roots having imbibed much of the atmosphere – and even more of the ale – of the mining community in which for so long he had lived. Because of his commitment to the rights of the common man and to ever larger pay packets he was known to all as Albert the Union. He called a spade a spade (at least). His political angularity was compensated for by a warm heart and a lively sense of humour. His humour took various forms from slapstick to doleful teasing. In the latter connection his favourite ploy at the very end of a deacon's meeting at which all had gone well was to say in sepulchral tones, 'I'm very worried about the subsidence under the vestry.'

Next to Albert the Union was the youngest deacon, Elwyn Roberts, the Deputy Headmaster of the all-age village school. Of lean and hungry look he was, at the same time (as Betty Pugh said one day), 'a bit flash', with his velvet-collared jacket, his drainpipe trousers, his winkle picker shoes and his quiffed hair. He was a radical in every way. It was said that he did not believe that God created the universe in six days. He was a pacifist. He was a vegetarian. To his fellow-deacon, Meirion Hughes, he was a sinister indoctrinator of the young. How could he have all these deficiencies against him and still be a deacon? Because his father, formerly of the village, had done well for himself in steel, and sent Dai Cashbox a cheque for £50 every year.

The fifth member of this noble band was the aforementioned Meirion Hughes. He was a widower of fifty-five, ginger-haired, dapper, waspish; yet in his close-set eyes the lamp of ardour still managed to gleam. He worked for the Council as a hygiene inspector, and the more rules and regulations there were, the better he was pleased. This legalistic attitude spilled over into his theology. Of all fundamentalists, he was the most fundamental. Indeed, it was rumoured that all the attempts to undermine flashy deacon Roberts had their source in him.

The most recent recruit to the diaconate was Mrs Rachel Morris of Lower Farm. Indeed, she had been elected only at the previous Church Meeting on the recommendation of the deacons. In the absence of a minister, Goronwy Rees having retired and died (well, the former because of the latter) on the same day six months ago, aged eighty-five, Jenkin Jones had conducted that meeting, which had been called specifically to consider the vacancy on the diaconate. Jenkin had offered a lengthy prayer by which, without doubt, all the needy in the world would have felt themselves encompassed, and had then introduced the business.

'Who shall it be, then?' However voluble he might have been in prayer, Jenkin Jones was always to the point in business.

With more bravado than good judgement, the radical Elwyn Roberts jumped in: 'I nominate Mrs Rachel Morris.'

Jenkin Jones was taken aback. Rachel's husband, Bill, was a rival farmer, and Jenkin's oldest enemy. Had he not allowed his pig slurry to run into Jenkins's field? Was he not for ever flaunting his new machinery – all of it bought on tick? But if Jenkin loathed Bill, he was terrified of Rachel. She was, to him (and readers will understand that these memoirs concern pre-politically correct times) all that the words 'Women's Institute' conjure up, magnified to infinity. But, he thought as he interpreted a meaningful glance from Dai Cashbox, without her cake stall at the annual Chapel Fayre there would be a sizeable gap in the chapel's income. So he composed himself:

'Any other suggestions or opinions?'

All went quiet. No theologian, and only a very intermittent Bible reader, Jenkin Jones was more than half expecting Meirion Hughes the fundamentalist to go in for some Bible punching. And it is true that Meirion was wrestling hard with himself. On the one hand, he knew that Paul had said that women should keep silence in church affairs. On the other hand, it was also true that Mrs Rachel Morris's daughter Shirley, still very attractive at forty-three, was the one on whom his narrowly set, ardour-filled eyes had fallen. And did not Ecclesiastes say that there was a time to keep silence?

Thus it was agreed to nominate Mrs Rachel Morris to the next Church Meeting. She gave her consent in the grudgingly humble, mock-modest way that is always expected, whilst inwardly feeling 'Now I've got those rascals where I want them', and was duly elected to the diaconate of Bethel.

So there they all were, with Elijah Morgan's fate, humanly speaking, in their hands. Dr Lewis opened the meeting with a prayer which had something to do with the way in which we are all encompassed by sublimities of ethereal beauty, eternal reality and incomprehensible magnitude about which we can say nothing; but he nevertheless kept droning on about them. Then came the business of the evening.

'First' said Dr Lewis (because Jenkin Jones had plonked a note written in block capitals right in front of him) 'it is my very great pleasure to welcome Mrs Rachel Morris to her first meeting as a deacon.' She blushed, fluttered her eyelids at him, and did her best to look demure. Looking demure was not really what Rachel was best at. Looking flamboyant was. She had dressed for the occasion, and was resplendent in a large, bright red hat and a new black suit with striking white lapels and pocket flaps. She needed what the fashion people call a generous fit, and with this out- fit all was properly contained and under control.

Said Jenkin Jones, 'I move that we recommend to the Church Meeting that a call be sent to Mr Elijah Morgan to become our minister.' He moved this not only to get things under way, not only because he had taken to Elijah Morgan, but also in the hope that very soon the drudgery of seeking a preacher for every Sunday would be over.

'Seconded,' said Mrs Rachel Morris in what was her maiden, and shortest ever, speech. The close-together eyes of Meirion Hughes alighted upon her, a wan smile playing upon his lips and a conservative theology tugging at his conscience, for the woman had spoken.

Then it all went quiet. Nobody said anything. After what seemed an eternity Albert the Union blurted out, 'Come on, everybody – this is where we can all stick our oar in!' This outburst brought even Dr Lewis down to earth, and he launched into a disquisition in which he contrasted the democracy of the trades unions in the Valleys and their devotion to majority rule, with the Congregational Way of seeking unanimity in Christ the only Lord of the Church. Most of this was lost upon Albert, and by way of arresting Dr Lewis's flow Jenkin Jones said, 'I think Mr Morgan seems a very pleasant chap.'

'So is A. J. Ayer,' retorted the teacher Elwyn Roberts, 'but I wouldn't want him to be my minister.' Elwyn was the first person in the village to own a television set, and he was addicted to *The Brains Trust*.

'He read his prayers,' thundered Meirion Hughes, adverting to the *bête noir* of many Nonconformists, who would much rather have the *same* 'extempore' ramble to the throne of grace each week than an intelligent use of written prayers.

'How do you know he read them?' asked Albert, 'were your eyes open?' and Meirion looked a little nonplussed. But he quickly recovered and tried another tack. 'He's not married,' he said, knowingly.

'What's that got to do with it?' asked Elwyn, who wasn't married either.

'Well, Mrs Rees was such a worker among the women,' said Meirion, 'and her home-made chocolates were renowned in hospitals far and wide.'

'I see,' snarled Elwyn, 'You want two for the price of one.'

Actually, what Meirion most wanted was Mrs Rachel Morris's daughter, Shirley, whose heart, he feared, might too readily incline towards a young, unmarried, minister – as sometimes happens.

'We could do with some youth about the place,' pronounced Mrs Morris, thinking to herself that at forty-two her Shirley might not be too late to catch Mr Morgan. 'Mr Rees was eighty-five when he died. This time we need someone young.'

Dr Lewis, ever alive to a dodgy argument, intervened: 'On a point of information, the late Mr Rees served here for sixty years, so last time you had a young minister.'

Through all of this Dai Cashbox had been weighing the pros and cons. True, an unmarried minister would not have an unpaid helper. On the other hand, an unmarried minister would not have two mouths to feed, so perhaps the stipend might usefully be reduced. And anything was better than Mrs Rees's chocolates. 'I vote we have him,' he blurted out.

'Not so fast,' said Meirion, 'his sermons weren't up to much.' Jenkin Jones trembled inwardly as he felt the onset of a theological harangue.

'What do you mean?' asked Elwyn: 'he seemed clear enough to me – quite inspiring in fact.'

'He didn't give us three points and a poem,' grumbled Meirion.

'But there's more than one way to plan a sermon,' retorted Elwyn.

'Mr Rees always gave us three points and a poem,' came the firm and frosty reply, 'and...'

By now Dai Cashbox had made a quick calculation. 'So that means', he said, 'that over sixty years we've had 18,720 points and 6,240 poems and I think that's enough for anybody. Let's have a change of pattern. Let's have Mr Morgan.'

'Hear! Hear!' cried Jenkin Jones, Elwyn Roberts and Rachel Morris in unison – and all for different reasons.

Albert the Union had been sitting quietly, looking troubled. 'What about you, Albert?' asked Dai.

'Is Mr Morgan a man of the people?' Albert wondered aloud, where-upon Elwyn began quietly to hum 'The Red Flag.' Then Elwyn said, 'More to the point, is he a pacifist?'

At this point, fearing the worst, Jenkin Jones said something really wise. 'We're all judging Mr Morgan according to our own likes and dis-likes. We'll never find a minister who agrees with all of us – nobody could, because we're usually at loggerheads with each other. The question is, can we rein in our prejudices, hold our tongues, unite behind Mr Morgan, and let him lead us forward?'

'Quite so,' said Dr Lewis, galvanised by the intuition that matters were coming to a head and that decision-time was nigh. 'Since none of the negative comments which have been made have the status of anything other than trifling, variously construed, particulars, and since our grand objective must be those universals towards which all right-minded souls tend (by now Albert was thinking, 'Get on with it – they'll be closing in five minutes!'); and furthermore, since there is not likely to be another candidate forthcoming in the near future (the colour drained from Jenkin Jones's face at the prospect), I shall put the motion to the vote – or rather (with a sudden recall of his theology) we shall seek the mind of Christ together forthwith. Is there a dissentient voice?'

Silence.

'That's that, then', said Jenkin.

'Not quite,' retorted Elwyn, glancing at Dai Cashbox, who knew what was coming. 'You can't call a minister if you cannot tell him about the terms and conditions he may expect.'

'Quite so,' said Meirion, in unaccustomed agreement with Elwyn. 'The labourer is worthy of his hire,' he continued piously – and would have said more, when Albert the Union, betraying his extra-ecclesial commit-ments, blurted out, 'What are the going rates?'

Albert had never heard – or if he had heard it, he had determinedly dismissed it – the distinction between a salary and a minister's stipend. But Dr Lewis, of course, had.

'The holy ministry is not to be considered in terms of hourly rates and closely specified duties,' he explained. 'Rather, a stipend is intended to free a minister from worldly care in order that he may perform the service to which he had been called.' As he paused for breath, Dai Cashbox intervened:

'We gave Mr Rees £280/10/6 per annum.'

'How long ago did we hit on that figure?' asked Elwyn.

'On his fiftieth anniversary with us,' Dai replied.

'More than ten years ago, then,' said Elwyn.

'By now,' said Jenkin, 'we should not give him less that £350. Any advance on that?' he added, thinking for a moment that he was at an auction – which, in a sense, he was.

'I say £360 because he's not your ordinary pastor, he's a BA of great promise, and if we go too low someone else will snap him up.' Thus spoke Albert the Union, ever sensitive to distinctions in pay and conditions.

Fearing that Albert might suddenly remember that by the time Mr Morgan came – if he did come – he would also most likely have a postgraduate BD degree, Dai Cashbox said, 'Done! £360 it is.'

'Is that the consensus of the meeting?' asked Dr Lewis. There being no dissentient voice, it was.

'And of course,' said Elwyn, 'he will have full use of the Manse.'

There was no difficulty about that. After all, none of them would have wanted to live in it, and it would be better to have it heated through the winter months.

Dr Iorwerth Lewis then said the benediction, adding the request that the serried ranks of the angelic host would smile upon them now and greet them joyfully when the good Lord called them home.

The deacons' recommendation that Mr Elijah Morgan be called to the pastorate, and that he receive a stipend of £360 per annum and full use of the Manse, was placed before the Church Meeting two days later, and carried unanimously. Indeed, so swiftly was the matter concluded that there was time for some hymns, three solos by Shirley Morris and a testimony (the same one as usual) from Meirion Hughes.

Then they all repaired to their homes – except Albert the Union, whose steps took him elsewhere – with the words of the hymn 'The ship of temperance' ringing in their ears.

2

Mr Elijah Morgan
is Ordained and Inducted

Except when pleading before the throne of grace Mr Jenkin Jones, as we know by now, was a man of few words. He was even less fluent as a writer of important letters. He had a pattern letter which he used when writing to the Tax Man in which he 'begged to point out' one or two things, and was always 'Yours most respectfully'. There were spaces in this pattern letter into which he inserted the current figures he was querying or seeking to explain away. He had another pattern letter that he used when writing to the bank manager for a loan. This one too had spaces: one for the object required – one year it was a tractor, another it was a barn extension – and another for the sum required. Jenkin hoped that the manager would be able to see his way to granting the request, and expressed the hope that the Sale of Work at the Parish Church (where the manager was a warden) would break all previous records. 'There's no need to creep,' Dilys had said on first reading this pattern letter some years before, but to date the letter had never failed, so Jenkin continued to wish financial blessings upon the Anglicans.

But now he had to write a letter for which he had no pattern at all. He realised that it would have to have a tincture of sanctity about it of a kind the bank manager did not need and the Tax Man would not have understood. It was a problem. Since the Revd Goronwy Rees had been at Bethel for sixty years, no ministers had been called since Jenkin was a lad; and his father, the previous church secretary, had taken no copies of 'call' letters which he had sent. There was nothing for it: he would have to sit down and put his mind to the job. And so he did:

Dear Mr Morgan,

Thank you very much for coming to take our services last Sunday. The Deacons met on Monday and they was unanimous that you should be our next minister. I took this recommendation to the Church Meeting on Wednesday, and they was unanimous too. So we think it's God's will that you come here. We hope you think so too. You will have £360/0/0 per annum plus full use of the Manse. We promise to look after you and support you in your work in this little corner of God's vineyard.

Looking forward to your reply,

Yours sincerely,

Jenkin Jones

'Whew', said Jenkin, as he laid down his pen. 'Is this alright, Dil?' he called out; and Dilys read the letter.

'That's lovely,' she said, and Jenkin breathed a sigh of relief. 'It's all true,' Dilys continued, 'it's to the point; and that last sentence is nice and religious. Shall I post it when I go to the shop?'

'Yes please,' said Jenkin, as he pulled on his boots in readiness for his more accustomed duties. As he walked across to the cowshed he thought, 'Good job I didn't have to put that letter before the deacons. Dai Cashbox would have seen pound notes attached to the phrase "We promise to look after you", and Meirion would certainly have wished to fling in a few biblical texts and a verse from a hymn.'

The letter was duly posted, and the very next morning (this being before advanced technology) Elijah received it at the Theological College. Now came his difficult piece of letter-writing. He had really taken to Bethel and its people. He felt that God wanted him there. He was delighted to have been called, but he must not write in such a way that it could be said that he had thought the call was a foregone conclusion. On the other hand he must not cross the boundary between humility and obsequious piety. So he wrote:

Dear Mr Jones,

Thank you very much for your letter of Thursday last. I very much enjoyed my visit to Bethel, and I thank you and all the members for the warm welcome I received. I am honoured that the church should have called me to be your next minister and, after prayerful consideration, I am pleased to accept your call and the terms as specified.

Please give my kind regards to all members. I look forward to being among you, and I am sure that with God's guidance we shall take great strides forward in His work.

God bless you all,
Elijah Morgan

The following Sunday, when giving out the notices, Mr Jenkin Jones asked the congregation to remain behind at the close of the service. There was a buzz of eager anticipation: what was it all about? Had the boiler burst again, and did the deacons want another special collection to put it right? Had the Walters twins been up to their mischief again in the graveyard? Had somebody died? (The discerning reader will note the order of these concerns in the minds of the good Christians of Bethel).

At the close of the service Jenkin Jones moved to the front. He stood there like an Old Testament prophet, his bald dome gleaming. He looked very happy. The congregation relaxed – especially the Walters twins: they hadn't been caught this time; the boiler must be safe, and nobody had died.

'Good news!' said Jenkin in his abrupt way. 'Mr Morgan is coming to be our minister.' Now Congregationalists do not clap in church, but if they did, they would have done so then. Everyone was delighted – so delighted that Jenkin felt quite a spoilsport as he continued …

'Now this means there's a lot of jobs to be done. We shall have to redecorate the Manse. It hasn't been done for years.' In fact, it hadn't been done since the twenty-fifth anniversary of the late Reverend Goronwy Rees's ministry, and that was about thirty-six years ago. 'It's bound to need a bit of touching up,' said Jenkin in what must have been the understatement of the year. The inside walls were faced with dark painted wood almost to shoulder height, and above was heavy wallpaper of the most sombre kind. There was that troublesome damp patch in the scullery, and the ceiling of the dining room was a maze of cracks resulting from the weight of the late Mr Rees's books which had been not only on shelves, but in heaps all over the floor in the study above. There was, indeed, much to be done.

'It'll cost the earth,' said Dai Cashbox, thinking of his sacred trust as treasurer. As soon as he said it, and knowing Jenkin of old, he realised that he had put his foot in it!

'That's why I think you should be in charge of a team of volunteers to get it done,' said Jenkin. Dai hated wallpapering, but he could not allow his reputation for frugality to be tarnished by any suggestion that they might seek a measure of professional assistance, so he reluctantly agreed. At once the women of the congregation began to think of all the odd rolls of wallpaper and offcuts of carpets they would be able to offload, while some of the men wondered how they could consistently claim that they had no head for ladder work when everyone knew that they tended their own gutters with no difficulty whatsoever.

'Then,' said Jenkin, 'there will have to be another team to tackle the Manse garden. It's a wilderness. Can you see to that, Elwyn?' Elwyn Roberts the school teacher was a great organiser, and a master of discipline. He could dragoon the most unruly bunch of tousled ten-year-olds into some sort of order, and he said he would have no difficulty marshalling a force to tackle the garden. Mrs Rachel Morris fixed on the word 'marshalling' and allowed herself a derisory sniff: 'Yes,' she whispered to Betty Pugh, 'that's about all he'll do – marshalling: he won't want to get his winkle-pickers dirty!'

The next thing Mrs Morris said was more charitable – and to the point. 'When we've got the Manse and garden ship-shape, what are we going to put in the Manse? It will be almost empty.'

'Mr Rees's bookcase will still be there,' said Jenkin.

'Thank God for that,' thought Albert the Union, thinking of his back. For the item in question was ten feet long and eight feet high. It had been a wedding present to Mr Rees and had been built in the Manse. Some rather unkindly said that Mr Rees had only stayed for sixty years because his beloved bookcase could not be removed unless the Manse were dismantled.

Fearing the worst, Dai Cashbox opined, 'Perhaps his parents will give him some furniture?'

'Maybe they will,' said Rachel, 'but we've got to show willing too.'

'There's that folding card table in the cubby hole off the Sunday School,' said Meirion. 'He could have that in the kitchen for the time being.'

'Agreed,' said Dai; and with that Meirion had achieved two goals: he had removed a devilish card table from divine precincts, and he would no longer pinch his fingers in the wretched thing when they needed to use it for special teas.

'And he could have a couple of wooden chairs from the Sunday School so that he can play cards with a mate in the kitchen,' volunteered Albert the Union.

As usual, Meirion bit: 'I pray the day may never come when our Manse will be used for card playing. It leads on to gambling, it ...' At this point he caught Mrs Morris's eye, and her piercing gaze was cautionary. Since, as we know, Meirion still had designs on her daughter, he stopped in full flight, whereupon she said, 'We can't just give him a load of junk. We must buy at least one nice item as a welcome gift from the church.'

Dai began to think of the smallest permissible item. A doormat? A garden rake? But Elwyn broke his reverie.

'Mr Morgan is going to need somewhere to sleep, and I propose we buy him a bed and some sheets and blankets. That would be a much appreciated gift, I'm sure.'

'That's a good idea,' said Jenkin quickly. He said it quickly, partly because he agreed, but mostly because he saw the look of alarm spreading across Dai Cashbox's face and thought it prudent to take the wind out of his sails.

'Will it be a single bed or a double?' asked Albert.

'He's not married,' blurted out Dai, 'why would he want a double bed?'

But Jenkin, thinking on the principle of the pot egg and the hen, said, 'Well we can't say that he won't get married, and we ought to be prepared in case he does.'

Dai was doing some rapid costings in his head. He calculated the difference in price between a single and a double bed; and then he calculated that if any future Mrs Morgan ran as good a cake stall as Mrs Rees had done, the difference in price between the two beds would be made up in three years.

'On second thoughts', said Dai, 'I agree with Jenkin. Let's give him a double bed and some bedding.'

As if capitalising on this conversion, Jenkin said, 'This need not be a charge on church funds: we can all chip in and it will be a gift from the deacons.' Dai was not sure whether he liked this idea, but he would not shame himself by saying so. Instead he said, 'Where shall we get the goods?'

Mrs Rachel Morris said, 'The obvious man to go to is Bus Fare Meredith in town. If you like, I will go and deal with him.'

The offer was gratefully accepted by the men, none of whom really felt that their vocation was amidst the beds and bedding in Bus Fare's shop. Dai Cashbox was particularly pleased, because his Betty had told him how Mrs Morris had 'dealt with' Bus Fare on a previous occasion: she got a season ticket's-worth knocked off the price.

Bus Fare Meredith was so called because once a week he sent one or two members of his Sunday School class to the larger town, Westford. In return for a bag of sweets and the bus fare they would peer through the windows of the furniture shops, noting the prices of major items. They would report back to Bus Fare, who would deduct the price of the return fare to Westford from the price he charged for the same items. In this way he kept trade local. 'Why spend the bus fare going there when I have the same item for less?' he would say. And thus his business blossomed.

'One more thing,' said Jenkin. 'We shall have to crank up the catering committee for the welcome tea. How about it, Mrs Morris?' The newest deacon, while not taking kindly to the idea of being cranked up, nevertheless graciously acceded to his request whilst thinking to herself, 'That will show Maude Evans!'

'That's about it, then,' said Jenkin. And as they were all about to go, Elwyn Roberts piped up: 'Excuse me, what about the most important thing of all?'

'What's that?' asked Jenkin.

'The ordination service, of course,' said Elwyn. 'Who will arrange that?'

Jenkin Jones, sensing that somehow he had managed to overlook the very item that was the point of all the rest, came over all bashful and blushed to the top of his dome. 'I – I – I,' he stuttered, at which point Albert the Union came to the rescue.

'Let the Union do it,' he said in stentorian tones.

Jenkin Jones momentarily had a vision of brass bands, marching miners and banners, and wondered what they had to do with ordinations. But then he gathered himself and remembered that they were, after all, part of a wider fellowship, and that it was sometimes convenient to remember this. Yes, the County Union was good at things like ordinations, and some of the officers would have to be invited anyway. And there was always the hope that if the service was long enough, the welcome tea heavy enough, and the speeches of welcome tedious enough the officials would be so exhausted at the end of it all that they would simply slope off to the big city without bothering to ask awkward questions about Bethel's unmet Union financial targets and the like.

'I shall telephone the secretary of the Union and ask him to arrange the service,' said Jenkin. And so it was.

The great day arrived. The Manse garden was looking a treat. The house itself had been painted outside and completely redecorated inside. The catering committee had been hard at work, and a special choir had been trained by Mrs Blodwen Llewellyn, LRAM. There had been no way of preventing Madame Myfanwy Price-Edwards from volunteering to sing 'All in an April evening' although it was late August; and Dai Cashbox said they shouldn't try because she was a highly sensitive artiste. His other reason, unexpressed, was that she had offered to pay for all the food at the welcome tea. This, of course, had caused more than a little tension between Dai and Shirley Morris, the regular soloist. But Dai promised he would work on Mr Morgan to give her an extra solo at the Carol Service, and thus the economics of the kingdom prevailed.

At 3.00 p.m. Bethel was bursting at the seams. Friends from neighbouring chapels had gathered as an expression of Christian fellowship and in order to sample Rachel Morris's Welsh cakes. Mr Morgan was there, of course, looking rather apprehensive – partly because of the challenge of the high calling he was about to embrace; partly because of concern lest his grandad's bladder gave out halfway through. For Elijah was well supported by relatives and friends from his home church on the other side of Wales.

Those taking part in the service filed in. Blodwen skilfully rounded off the voluntary halfway through. The organ emitted a wheeze as of one expiring, and the service began.

The Reverend Dr Iorwerth Lewis conducted the service. He opened with a statement about the meaning of ordination, but soon lost everybody by musing on the contributions to the subject of Clement, Eusebius, John Damascene and others who, whoever they were, were all from the other side of Offa's Dyke.

The hymns went well – especially Philip Doddridge's hymn of consecration,

> My gracious Lord, I own Thy right
> To every service I can pay…

How lustily the denominational dignitaries and those princes of the pulpit who could command the biggest preaching fees sang the verse which goes,

> I would not breathe for worldly joy,
> Or to increase my worldly good,
> Nor future days or powers employ
> To spread a sounding name abroad.

Between that verse and the next Albert the Union was heard to mutter, 'Pull the other one' – for which expostulation he received a sharp nudge in the ribs from Ada.

Jenkin Jones the secretary was called out to give an account of the steps leading to the call. He recounted the prayerful and sensitive way in which the deacons had considered the pastoral vacancy …

'He must have been at a different meeting from me,' muttered Albert, receiving a further nudge from Ada.

Jenkin explained how hard it had been for Christ's little flock [they were 'Christ's little flock' today in the presence of visitors; but on other occasions, when cheerful he knew them as 'the gang', and when in despair, as 'the mob'] without a regular minister. People drifted away…

'And the money goes down,' interjected Dai Cashbox.

'Anyway,' says Jenkin, 'it's all right now. The Lord has provided. Our prayers have been answered.' He was about to say, 'We think we've picked a good 'un' when he bethought himself and revised this to: 'We thank the

Lord for leading us to a good man, and a scholar too – BA and BD.' For Elijah had indeed passed his final BD examinations, and with flying colours too. 'Even though Mr Morgan isn't married,' Jenkin continued, 'I expect he'll do well enough. In any case he'll have us to keep him in order.'

As all of this assailed his ears Mr Elijah Morgan reflected that he had seldom heard such a mixture of sentiments at once so worldly and so godly. Was the church secretary simply a less-than-fully-consistent hypocrite? Or was he one genuinely on the road to sanctification but ever at risk of being dragged down by what the apostle Paul called his 'old man'?

Before he had time to decide the issue Dr Iorwerth Lewis was announcing the choir item. Mercifully – perhaps because even he could find no link between it and the Pseudo-Dionysius – he made no attempt to explain why anyone should have thought that a spirited rendering of 'John Brown's Body' was deemed liturgically appropriate on such a solemn occasion as this.

Following this shaking of the rafters, the Reverend Eli Lloyd reverently mounted the pulpit steps. He was short, chubby, with a beatific smile on a countenance topped by flowing locks of white hair. He was Mr Elijah Morgan's home minister, and he had known the ordinand all his life. He had baptised him; he had received him as a church member; he had encouraged him to become a Sunday School teacher. He was sure that Mr Morgan would be an adornment to any church. Mr Lloyd tactfully failed to mention that on one occasion he had caught Elijah and the lads having a smoke behind the vestry after a Band of Hope meeting.

Then Elijah Morgan himself went to the pulpit to give his statement of faith. He had sweated over it for many hours. It was a statement on the basis of which those hearers with particularly acute doctrinal antennae would judge him for the rest of his days. So it had to be right. He stood there, took a deep breath (forgetting what the Theological College's voice specialist had said about the air's being there already), and began. His eye caught that of Meirion Hughes the fundamentalist just as he was about to say that he believed that the Bible *contained* the Word of God. He said it anyway, and Meirion scowled and muttered, 'Liberal weasel word! The Bible *is* the Word of God.'

So concerned had Elijah been about his statement of faith that he had submitted the fifth draft of it to Principal Morgan MacDonald. It had come back with red ink marks all over it. 'Here you sail too close to Arminianism.' 'They will think you are a fellow-traveller with the Unitarians if you say this.' 'Are you trying to upset the Roman Catholics?' Most damning of all, the one word, 'Heresy!!' Elijah made his corrections and now, with Dr MacDonald beaming up at him, he pressed on.

Next, the act of ordination and the prayer. This was in the hands of the Reverend Idris Llewellyn, secretary of the County Union, representing the wider family of Congregational churches. It was also his task to gather in the sums levied upon all the churches in accordance with their membership. As Mr Llewellyn stood at the front, addressing the formal questions to Elijah Morgan, Dai Cashbox bent down in his pew as if to tie his shoe lace. He did not wish to have eye contact with Mr Llewellyn lest the latter were prompted to recall how long it was since a cheque had come his way from Bethel. Dai did not wish the Union Secretary to have such mercenary thoughts during an ordination service – or, indeed, at any other time.

Madame Myfanwy Price-Edwards then swept to the front of the chapel. Of indeterminate age and ample proportions, she was now to render her solo. She positioned herself close to Blodwen at the organ, and let rip on 'Bless this house' to such a degree that had she been singing in the Royal Albert Hall people on the pavement outside would have reached for their ear-plugs. Blodwen knew her of old, of course, and her ear-plugs were already in situ. After all, Bethel was not a large chapel.

Madame Price-Edwards had the widest vibrato for miles around – it extended over three semitones, and she was very proud of it. On one occasion at a local eisteddfod an adjudicator had dared to call it a wobble! She never graced an eisteddfod platform again. But, as on this occasion, she had ways of being invited to sing in chapels. Paying for the tea was only one of them, for she was a notorious gossip, and on more than one occasion, by allowing her to open her mouth in song a good Christian soul had managed to keep it shut concerning more incendiary matters.

The solo over, up into the pulpit strode the genial Principal Dr Morgan MacDonald of the Theological College. His very name was a sign of the eccentric mixture that he was. His grandfather had come down from Scotland to work in the mines; his father, also a miner, had never forgiven him for taking to book learning ('A right namby-pamby way of life,' he had declared); and when, shortly after the First World War, Morgan had gone off to study in *Germany*, his father had completely written him off. Such tensions, combined with his innate oddities, made him a theological teacher whose eccentricities would be rehearsed by generations of ministers to come. He was an authority on John Calvin and sweet peas. His students had long since learned that the best way of diverting him from the doctrine of predestination was to ask how his hybrids were doing. Then his face would light up, he would forget all about the fate of the impenitent wicked, and he was away until the bell went.

Today Principal MacDonald was addressing the charge to the minister and to the church. He exhorted the Reverend Elijah Morgan (for, being now ordained, he was correctly addressed thus) to be diligent in study, faithful in pastoral visitation, and earnest in preaching and in prayer. He urged the church members to play their utmost part in the life of the church; to devote all their energies to the cause ...

'Some of us have got a living to make,' thought Sam Jones, momentarily forgetting that he had been on the dole for ages.

Then, far away, as if surrounded by the prophets, apostles and martyrs of the ages, the Principal's face lit up and he reached a grand conclusion replete with untranslated quotations in Hebrew, Latin and German.

'He's just as far above our heads as Dr Lewis,' whispered Ada Williams to Mary Smith.

'At least Dr Lewis is above our heads in our own language,' Mary whispered back.

After the final hymn and blessing, the welcome tea.

They all filed into the tiny schoolroom. The tables groaned under the weight of Welsh cakes, Bara Brith, drop scones, and sandwiches. So many were the guests that the Congregationalists had had to humble themselves and borrow the Baptists' tea urn. Meirion Hughes, deacon and hygiene inspector, was worried. He had spotted so many violations of regulations and good practice that it was as much as he could do to wolf down three helpings of everything on offer.

When everyone was sated, speeches of welcome were made. First, the Rector of the Anglican parish, the Reverend Aneurin Bentley-Jones.

He was one of those Anglicans who compensated for the sketchiest of theological educations by being well bred. He looked like a prosperous farmer – indeed, he was also a prosperous farmer. He knew a great deal about the ills which befell ancient stone buildings, and the Bishop found him very useful. When he was not inspecting church buildings he rode to hounds. And when he was not doing either (which was not often), he made his pastoral calls. These were also influenced by his interest in buildings, and his preferred scene of pastoral visitation was a home that had a minimum of eight bedrooms and a good cellar. The fact that the Church in Wales was disestablished in 1920 had never really impinged upon his consciousness, and he always treated 'Nonconformists' in the patronising, disdainful way he reserved for all who were 'below stairs.' But he was there, and he managed the kind of greeting which made the Reverend Elijah Morgan feel that although he had taken a denominational wrong turning, and belonged to a lesser breed, he had not thereby entirely forfeited a place in the kingdom of heaven.

The other greeting – there was only one other because the local Baptist pastor, the Reverend Calvin Rowlands, a high Calvinist whose sermons bore a striking resemblance to those of Charles Haddon Spurgeon, was quite sure that the Congregationalists were very far from the kingdom, and accordingly feared contamination and refused fellowship. The other greeting was from the Reverend J. Wesley Protheroe. His name at once betrayed him as a Methodist, though the Reverend Elijah Morgan knew him as plain Joe Protheroe – how many Methodist ministers suddenly became 'The Reverend Initial Wesley Something' on ordination, he mused. Elijah had wanted to get even with Joe for ages, and for two reasons. First, because of the foul. Every year the Methodist and Congregational Colleges met on the soccer field. Two years before Elijah was the Congregational inside right, and Protheroe was a Methodist full back. As Elijah approached the Methodist goal, Protheroe fouled him. There was no doubt about it. It was a wicked act. But the referee didn't see it – he was a Unitarian: what could you expect? And the Congregationalists lost the match.

Secondly there was the time when Elijah and some of his pals raided the Methodist College and kidnapped the bust of John Wesley from the entrance hall. It turned out afterwards that it was the sanctimonious Joe Protheroe who had named Elijah as the chief conspirator to the completely humourless Principal Roderick Perkins. It was never entirely clear to the Congregationalists whether Principal Perkins was more incensed because John Wesley had been kidnapped, which was a mere crime, or because he had later been found in an unused toilet in the grounds of the Congregational College, which was sacrilege.

There stood the Reverend J. Wesley Protheroe, oozing sanctity as only a Methodist could (though Elijah remembered what Joe had called him on the soccer field. It was not complimentary, and John Wesley would not have been pleased).

'I am,' says Protheroe, 'but a lowly representative of the people called Methodists. I am the junior circuit minister. Above me is the circuit superintendent minister, and above us both is the Methodist Conference which is, under God, our supreme authority.'

'The creep,' thought Elijah. 'Joe's got his eye on a plum circuit. Jabez Bunting, that clerically-minded Methodist organiser of the nineteenth century, would have been proud of him – except that he would probably have crossed out the words "under God".' Elijah immediately repented of having such unworthy thoughts during his ordination service. He focused again on what Protheroe was saying and could hardly believe his ears …

'I look forward to many happy years of co-operation in this district with the Reverend Elijah Morgan, my longstanding friend, your minister. May showers of blessing attend his efforts, may you all be richly blessed under his leadership, and may the Lord's cause enjoy a season of refreshing which shall redound to his praise and glory.'

The Reverend Elijah Morgan felt sick.

There being no more speeches, Dr Iorwerth Lewis thanked the ladies at length – he was quite sure that the serried ranks of angels themselves would have had their palates tickled by the fare so generously provided. They sang the Doxology, and they all went home.

Jenkin Jones and Dai Cashbox were the last to leave. Said Dai, 'Not one of those denominational snoopers had a chance to get a word in about the money.' It had truly been a most successful occasion.

3

The Reverend Elijah Morgan
Settles In

After the excitements of the weekend – ordained on Saturday, first Sunday in pastoral charge – the Monday might have seemed flat. The party from Elijah's home church had returned in their coach; his church members had returned to their daily rounds and common tasks; the cock at the next-door farm had tired of crowing, there being no more humans to awaken; and it was very quiet. But Elijah was wide awake and excited. He was wide awake because, with the threatening encouragement of Mrs Rachel Morris, Bus Fare Meredith had supplied a most comfortable double bed and Elijah had enjoyed the best two nights' sleep of his life. He was excited because, apart from the exhausting hike up the hill with young Adrian Pugh, this was the first opportunity he had had to explore the neighbourhood.

Having no option but to walk, he set off at a brisk pace to the village. On his left was the field which surrounded Bethel and its Manse; on his right were two cottages originally built for farm labourers. At the junction he turned right and headed towards the village. There were more fields on his right, but on his left was an area of deciduous woodland. The leaves had only just begun to suggest their autumn colours, and as yet posed no threat to the magnificent display of foxgloves, still in flower. '*Digitalis purpurea*,' mused Elijah, for Latin had been among his BA subjects, and it was a language he loved.

Another half mile, and there was the village of Bethel. On the outskirts were five or six council houses, most of which had a garden shed, and one or two had greenhouses; and another farm. There were two or three large dwellings standing in their own grounds, and then came the Parish

33

Church of St Mary. It had a tall, tapering tower typical of the area, which in past centuries had served as a defence and a lookout. Elijah walked through the graveyard towards the open door. The notice board indicated that Matins were at 11.00 and Evensong at 6.30. There was no reference to any weekday activities, and those requiring baptisms or weddings were instructed to telephone the Churchwarden on 406. As far as the notice-board was concerned the Rector was conspicuous by his absence – a condition that aptly described his general relationship to the parish.

Elijah went in. The interior was in the shape of a slightly 'drunken' rectangle, to which at some point a transept had been added. The furnishings were simple, and everything was tidy. But there was that slight musty smell which often goes with old churches near the sea. The font was Norman, and there were two candlesticks on the altar. The two-manual organ needed two pairs of hands: one to play it, one to pump it. There was a single bell rope. On the table by the door was a Visitors Book, slightly warped by the damp. Elijah noticed that most of the recent visitors were from other parts of the county, a few from neighbouring counties, and one was from Rotherham. Half way down the current page was the intimation, clearly in a teenager's hand, that a Dick Barton of Devil's Gallop had recently visited the church. To a wireless-lover like Elijah the cleverness of the anonymous youth in knowing the title of Charles Williams's signature tune to the popular programme, *Dick Barton – Special Agent*, more than compensated for any sacrilege done to the Visitors Book.

Turning left out of the churchyard, Elijah passed a number of houses and bungalows on either side of the road. Many were grey stucco, others were colourwashed in cream or pale pink. On the right was the garage owned by Derek Hart. A skilled mechanic, it was said that he could mend anything; and certainly more than one farmer in the vicinity had had cause to thank Derek for staving off the evil day when he would have to put his hand in his pocket and fork out for some expensive new machinery. Not, indeed, that Derek was infallible. On the patch of land adjoining the garage were the remains of vehicles of many types that he had not been able to save. These corpses he plundered for parts until their shells were of no further use. He would then call in Tinker Joe (whose rightly ordered name was Joseph Tinker, but whose profession equated with his surname), and Tinker Joe would come along with faithful Dobbin and cart, gather up the metallic remains, and transport them to the scrapyard in town. Tinker Joe lived in a gypsy caravan with Rowena, his wife, and five children – all of them well known to Elwyn Roberts for that combination of mischief and worldly-wisdom characteristic of budding kings of the road.

Derek's garage was really a glorified hut. He had taken it over from his father who, in turn, had inherited it from his father who in those days had been a wheelwright. But now it had an inspection pit, tool racks and a bench inside, while the outside was adorned with tin commercial advertisements proclaiming such truths as 'Motorist wise Simonize.' Two petrol pumps graced the tiny forecourt. As Elijah approached the garage, Derek emerged from the inspection pit. He was a cheerful man of about forty-five. He wore overalls, and his hands bore the greasy traces of his trade.

'Hello, I know who you are,' he called out; and Elijah went over to him.

'I'm very pleased to meet you,' said Elijah, 'though I'm afraid I won't be able to boost your trade very much. As you can see, I'm on Shanks's pony.'

'Not even a bike?' asked Derek.

'Afraid not,' said Elijah.

'Well, I'll have to put my thinking cap on about you,' said Derek. 'Meantime come round the back and see my idol.' He thought the new minister had a twinkle in his eyes, so it would be safe to try a religious allusion. He had tried it once with the Reverend Calvin Rowlands. Not only did his quip go down like a lead balloon with that straight-laced soul, but Rowlands said, 'I shall pray for you' – and that hurt!

Around the back they went, and there stood Derek's beautifully restored 1930 Jowett 7. It had four doors and four seats. Its seats looked really comfortable and Elijah was overjoyed when Derek said, 'Shall we go for a spin?'

'Have you got time?' asked Elijah.

'Plenty. I'm the boss, and if somebody is desperate for petrol while we're out they'll probably wait. The next pump is five miles away.'

So off they went. The car held the road well, and its finger-indicators popped out promptly when summoned. Always glad of a captive audience, Derek regaled Elijah with innumerable details as to the car's insides.

At the end of the trip Elijah was ashamed to realise that the only detail he could remember was that the car's capacity was 907 cc. He fervently hoped that Derek would not test him on the subject; and he did not. In fact, on returning they found Tinker Joe and Dobbin on the garage forecourt. Tinker Joe was contentedly puffing his pipe and weighing up what price he would get for the metal on the rough land by Derek's garage. Dobbin was equally contentedly munching on the contents of his nosebag.

'Now then, Tinker Joe,' said Derek, 'how's tricks?'

'All's well,' replied the tinker.

'This here is the new Bethel minister, Mr Morgan,' said Derek.

'Pleased to meet you, young sir,' said Tinker Joe as he shook Elijah's hand so vigorously that he nearly pulled his arm from its socket. 'Mind you,' he said quickly, 'I'm not much of a one for your line of business. My religion's more about looking after the good earth. That's why me and Dobbin roam over the countryside removing scrap and suchlike.'

Elijah thought that this was a strangely pious motivation, especially at a time when scrap prices were known to be high. Elijah said, 'I quite understand. But if ever I can be of service to you and your family, don't hesitate to ask.'

By now Tinker Joe was really warming to Elijah. 'First I shall serve you,' he said. 'You finish your rounds while I load this scrap from Derek's, and then you come to my vardo, have a cup of tea and meet my Rowena.'

'Thank you very much,' said Elijah. 'But where are you parked?'

'Take the next turn to the left, and we're in the third field down on the right.'

With that he turned to Derek, said, 'Let's get on with it then,' and the two of them made off as Elijah called out, 'Thanks Derek; see you soon, Tinker Joe.'

Elijah continued through the village. He passed the police house, but Constable Powell was clearly not there: the place looked deserted. It would have been natural to think that he was out on his rounds making this rural fastness secure against hardened criminals. But Elijah had already learned that the greatest challenges to Bethel's officer of the law were presented by the notorious Walters twins. They had graduated from putting drawing pins on the chair of Mrs Beatrice Jarman the Sunday

School teacher to a variety of more sinister activities. On one occasion, it was said, when the bracken on the hill was at its driest and most brittle, they had set fire to it, hid amongst the gorse and checked Constable Powell's response time on their watches. It was a blisteringly hot day, and PC Powell had to abandon his sit-up-and-beg bike near the foot of the hill and struggle up the incline as fast as he could. His normally rubicund features became dangerously scarlet, his breath came in short bursts, and sweat poured down from under his helmet. He had had the presence of mind to call the part-time firemen, and they had responded as swiftly as their daily work would permit. Constable Powell strongly suspected the Walters twins, but he had no hard evidence. He took some small satisfaction, however, from the fact that Mr Eryl Walters's day had been disrupted, for he was both the father of the twins and the team leader of the part-time firemen. Happily, no great damage was done, though when the postman, George Cadwallader, told Professor Gareth Reynolds about it the following morning, the Professor lamented, 'Do those boys never think about the insects?' For Professor Reynolds was a world-renowned entomologist who, though officially retired, had never ceased to scrabble amongst the leaf mould and rotting trees of the Bethel neighbourhood.

Opposite the police house was the school – an all-age establishment presided over by Mr Daniel Thomas. A rotund personage, he was very short and, consistently, he had a very short fuse. In a word, he was 'old school'. His eyes would almost pop out of his head at the slightest misdemeanour; he would clench his teeth; and more often than not he would rasp, 'Where are they?' Within minutes the backsides of the Walters twins would be on the other end of his cane. Although he was a Unitarian, he never stopped at one where caning was concerned. On the contrary, he often exceeded eight, the number of clauses in his beloved Racovian Catechism. Elwyn Roberts the deacon was his Deputy Head, and in charge of Music and Drama throughout the school. No two colleagues could have been more unlike in character and teaching method. Where Daniel ruled by fear, Elwyn caught the pupils' interest with exciting presentation. Where Daniel was formally, even stuffily, dressed, Elwyn, as we know, was an arbiter of the latest London fashion. One look at Elwyn at interview would have put Daniel off him whatever his teaching skills might have been but, providentially, Elwyn was in post before Daniel came. What is more Daniel's predecessor, John Norris, who had had Daniel on his staff in another school, and who loathed him, appointed Elwyn as his Deputy Head just three months before he retired, and after Daniel had been appointed to succeed him. 'That'll settle his hash!' Norris muttered to himself as his face broke into a leer.

The one remaining place on the village street for Elijah to visit was the shop. Bethel Village Stores was in the capable hands of Hetty Bevan. Hetty was a member of Horeb Baptist Chapel, but that did not matter. Why could it conceivably have mattered? Well, as Elijah knew from Professor Geraint Jenkins's pastoral theology lectures, 'Half a pound of butter can lose you members.' And the Professor went on to recount how, in his first pastorate, he had bought half a pound of butter from a grocer's shop run by Methodists, and not from one a few yards further on, the proprietor of which was one of his deacons. Word got out, the deacon resigned, taking his family with him. But everyone would understand that it was quite in order for Elijah to shop at Hetty's because there was no other shop for more than three miles in any direction.

Elijah opened the shop door, and this action operated a loud bell. He walked in, and as he did so Hetty came in from the storeroom at the back. She was a large, jolly person – so cheerful that Elijah wondered how she could tolerate the hardline Calvinism of the Reverend Calvin Rowlands. She did not give the impression of one whose thoughts had been unduly disturbed by the doctrine of total depravity on which, it was said, Mr Rowlands dwelt so long and so frequently.

'Welcome to my treasure trove!' chirrupped Hetty. 'And welcome to Bethel. I hope you'll be very happy among us.'

'I'm sure I shall be,' said Elijah. 'And thank you for coming to my ordination service – I saw you sitting at the back.' In a chapel the size of Bethel one would have needed particularly deficient eyesight not to have seen Hetty, for she was a 'presence'.

'Yes,' she said. 'It was a lovely service too. I do wish our Mr Rowlands had been there. But he has his principles. And I have *mine*,' she said, with great emphasis. Elijah believed her. In any case, being the proprietor of the only shop in the village she had no need to speak in such a way as to prevent custom from going elsewhere; and being a good Baptist she would not have dreamed of doing so even if the commercial circumstances had been different.

'Mr Rowland did pray for you the Sunday before your service,' she continued.

'I suppose he asked God to make me see the light,' said Elijah, breezily. Hetty's face fell. 'I'm afraid he did,' was her crestfallen reply. 'He also warned us not to attend. But I thought, "Blow him!" so I came – and without a disguise too. If your ordination had been around Christmas I could have come as Father Christmas, but everyone would still have known it was me.' Then, remembering the objective of her business she asked, 'Can I get you something?'

'Well, this morning I'm just trying to get my bearings, so if you don't mind, I'd like to look around the shop to see what you have.'

'Lovely job,' said Hetty. 'You look round for five minutes while I go and make us a cup of tea.' Just come up the stairs in the storeroom and you'll find my living quarters.' Off she bustled, and Elijah had the shop to himself.

What an emporium it was! When stocking it Hetty seemed to have thought of everything that anyone in the area might need, and quite a few things that they would never need. She still had a souvenir of the Festival of Britain, and a Hovis Coronation periscope, but in other ways she was up to the mark. Among the washing powders there was Persil, which had not long ago been launched, and was rapidly putting Fab in its place. She even had those new-fangled Tetley tea bags, which Elijah had found so useful in College, but which the ladies of the Bethel catering committee despised in favour of what they called 'a proper drink of tea'. Casting his eye around Elijah could see Dinky toys, jigsaw puzzles, breakfast cereals – including his favourite, Force; cheese, wellington boots, vegetables – turnips and swedes being prominent among them; paraffin lamps, mousetraps, socks, stockings, and lipstick by Max Factor with pictures of Ava Gardner and Elizabeth Taylor on the advertisement for it. As might have been expected, Meirion Hughes had a great interest in lipstick and all things cosmetic. Not that he wanted to purchase such things; rather, that he wanted to banish them from the land. Whenever he paid his periodic visits to Hetty's shop in his Council hygiene inspector capacity, he would moan about 'painted women' and the way they led innocent men astray, and he would ask Hetty whether sales of the 'junk' were rising or falling. Her answer always disappointed him.

There were rakes and hoes, and a cabinet of small drawers containing nails and screws, nuts and bolts. There were bottles of Corona, Dr Collis Brown's Chlorodyne, and Fiery Jack by Pickles of Yorkshire – that rubbing cream which Elijah's grandad always swore was so fierce that it made you quite forget the muscle pains you started with. Among the sweets he saw the newly marketed Spangles and another of his grandad's favourites: Uncle Joe's Mint Balls. Elijah's grandad, though he had never been out of Wales, was a fund of miscellaneous information, and he often used to say that the only two things Wigan was famous for were Uncle Joe's Mint Balls and George Formby.

But what most interested Elijah were the newspapers and magazines, for he was a great reader. Almost all the London papers were there on a stand – except the *Daily Worker*. Hetty had but one customer for the communist paper – Albert the Union – and she kept his favourite journal hidden under the counter as if it were the epitome of all things pornographic. The *News Chronicle* was by far the most popular daily paper amongst Hetty's customers, though she always reserved the *Daily Telegraph* for the Rector and the *Manchester Guardian* for Elwyn Roberts. Not surprisingly, the *Farmer's Weekly* was prominently displayed, and alongside it the *Farmer and Stockbreeder*. Nearby was that green-covered quarterly, *The Countryman*, read by so many who preferred to think about things rural rather than to work among them. *Picture Post, Illustrated, Everybody's Weekly* and *John Bull* competed with one another for those readers who liked solid reading matter well illustrated by photographs. For those with lighter tastes there were *Answers* and *Tit-Bits*. Those who sought humorous prose could find it in *Lilliput*, while the *Strand Magazine* carried a variety of fiction.

Elijah was pleased to see that some of the comics he had enjoyed as a boy had found their way to Hetty's shop. There was *Champion* – how he had enjoyed the tales of Rockfist Rogan; and there was *Wizard*, which had run a most entertaining serial story about Johnny Appleseed. For girls there was *Girls Crystal*, and for younger children, *Playbox* and *Rainbow*, *Radio Fun* and *Film Fun*. Of *Chips* there was no sight, for that venerable comic had recently ceased publication, and Elijah reflected that the world would be a slightly sadder place without the exploits of Weary Willie and Tired Tim. By way of compensation, there was the recently launched comic, *The Eagle*, with its tales of Dan Dare, and *Dandy* and *Beano* were much in evidence. But what pleased him most was that the *Boy's Own Paper* was still going strong. This magazine had come to the Morgan family ever since it was founded in 1879 by the Religious Tract Society. Elijah's grandad remembered the contributions by the Reverend J. G. Wood on nature study and, indeed, he had two of that worthy's books: *Half Hours in Field and Forest*, and *Birds of the Bible*. These books were approved for reading in Grandad's house on Sundays, as was *Christie's Old Organ* – Mrs Walton's tale of the orphan boy who was instrumental in the conversion of Old Treffy the organ grinder, whose organ played only one tune, 'Home, sweet home'. Elijah was pleased to see that Captain W. E. Johns's daring pilot, Biggles, was still up to his exploits in the *Boy's Own Paper*; and, Latinist that he was, he thought that over many years the magazine had been true to its motto, *Quicquid agunt pueri nostri farrago libelli*.

But the largest pile of papers comprised the *Newbridge Sentinel*. This was edited by Mr Arnold Jackson. It was a mine of information of interest to anyone within eight miles of town. Mr Jackson was a staunch Presbyterian, who had some Scottish blood in his veins. Thus, even though the Welsh Anglicans had been disestablished in 1920, he still regarded them as an English, bishop-ridden sect quite unlike the Church of Scotland. For this reason he invariably 'lost' the visit of the Bishop among the results of the local darts matches on the back page, whereas the least newsworthy Nonconformist items would claim banner headlines: MAUNDER'S OLIVET TO CALVARY A SELL-OUT AT PENUEL; or ANGHARAD MATTHIAS WINS HEPHZIBAH'S CAKE PRIZE FOR THE THIRD TIME.

Underneath the paper's title was the claim, 'Circulation ever increasing', though the contents seemed to give the lie to this. For a large part of the paper consisted of reports of funerals with everyone attending listed, and the number of ministers present particularly noted. Sometimes a minister would remonstrate with Mr Jackson: 'If you report my funeral oration so fully, I shall not be able to use it again!' And sometimes the Letters page was almost entirely filled by missives from those aggrieved by the fact that their names had been omitted from the lists of mourners.

'Tea's ready!' called out Hetty; and Elijah went into the back room and up the stairs. As he entered the living room he had the shock of his life. The room was not large; it was crowded with furniture; but almost every inch of the wall was covered by framed prints of cats by Louis Wain. Hetty saw that Elijah was somewhat taken aback.

'I love my cats,' she said, rather unnecessarily.

'So I see, said Elijah.'

There were smiling cats, angry cats, half-crazed cats, regal cats, priestly cats, cheeky cats, professional cats – in fact, every kind of cat you could think of.

'How long have you been collecting these?' Elijah asked.

'For twenty years,' Hetty replied; 'ever since your Meirion came inspecting and said I must not have my five cats roaming around a food shop.

Elijah saw the point, and he took 'your' in 'your Meirion' to have a denominational, not a personal, reference.

They drank their tea, had a good chat, and then the shop bell went. So Hetty went about her business, and Elijah continued on his way. He turned right out of the shop, and left at the next road junction. And, sure enough, there in the third field on the right was Tinker Joe's caravan, or vardo. The sun was shining full on it, and it was a glorious sight. It was beautifully decorated in traditional style, and from its chimney there came the aroma of something appetising being cooked on the Queen's stove below. By its side stood Dobbin, and the cart with its load of scrap metal.

As Elijah approached the vardo Tinker Joe appeared at the door. Behind him was Rowena. They came down the wooden steps and greeted Elijah as if he were a long-lost cousin.

'Welcome, welcome,' said Tinker Joe; 'Meet my Rowena.' Rowena was an attractive woman; her deportment was admirable: indeed, there was something regal about her. She was neatly attired in a long black dress with a traditionally embroidered bodice. Her black hair was swept into a bun at the back. While Tinker Joe was searching for scrap, she would make the meals, look after the children, clean the vardo, make and sell clothes pegs in the late autumn and winter, and work in local fields and market gardens during the summer months.

'What do you think of our palace?' asked Tinker Joe.

Elijah was full of admiration for it. 'It's a work of art,' he said, and so it was.

'It's called a Reading,' said Tinker Joe, 'because Reading is where it was made. The back wheels are five feet high, the front ones three foot six. The side walls slope outwards a little, and between the wheels and under the floor there is storage space.'

'What's that on the top?' asked Elijah.

'We call that a mollicroft,' came the reply. 'It's a raised section of the roof with little windows on either side. It gives us a bit more light.'

At this point Rowena came to the doorway and said, 'Tea's ready.' So up the steps they went. There was no question that Rowena was an admirable housekeeper. The place was spotless. Opposite the door, running from side to side of the vardo at chest height was the bed, extendable to double size. Below it were sleeping places for the children. The stove was on the right, so that its chimney would not be at risk from overhanging trees when on the road. To the left were a wash basin, cupboards and a table. On every free piece of wall space hung Rowena's collection of porcelain plates. But the item she treasured most was her Crown Derby twin-handled urn with its beautifully decorated lid. This stood on a special shelf that Tinker Joe had made for it. Altogether the vardo made a compact and cosy home, and Tinker Joe and Rowena were clearly very proud of it.

'There's five types of wood in this vardo,' Tinker Joe declared: 'pine, oak, walnut, ash and elm.'

By now they were sitting on stools at the table. Rowena had made mugs full of tea, and they chatted away happily. Then she said, 'What would you like to eat?'

'Oh,' stammered Elijah, 'I couldn't possibly trouble you for food.'

'Nonsense,' retorted Rowena. 'Even parsons have to eat. Have you got something cooking at home?'

For the first time that morning Elijah realised that he had not. He had been entertained in one way or another all over the weekend, but now he was on his own. And he suddenly remembered that he had not even lit the Rayburn before coming out.

'Well, no, I haven't,' he said, whereupon Rowena as if by magic whisked out bread, butter and cheese from her larder, and they all tucked in.

At last it was time for Elijah to leave.

'Before you go, said Tinker Joe, Rowena and me has a little treat for you.' Elijah wondered what it could be, but Rowena gave her husband a knowing look.

'You go down to that bit of hard standing outside the vardo,' said Tinker Joe, and Elijah did as requested. Half a minute later Tinker Joe led Rowena down the steps of the vardo and onto the hard standing. In one hand he had a bow, in the other a violin.

'Ready?' he asked Rowena.

'Yes,' she replied.

With that, Tinker Joe broke into 'The rakes of Mallow,' and Rowena danced beautifully in time to his accomplished playing from memory. Elijah was amazed that Tinker Joe's fingers, so worn by humping lumps of metal around, could move so swiftly and with such precision as he bowed his beloved fiddle, holding it not under his chin, but between his left hand and his shoulder. Elijah applauded them enthusiastically, and thanked them warmly for their hospitality and for the entertainment. In an attempt to honour both his calling to evangelism and the inbred suspicion of churches which he knew some travelling folk to have, he simply said, 'Don't hesitate to let me know if I can help you at any time.'

'We will,' they said, as they waved him off.

Elijah turned right out of the field and almost at once the narrow road began to rise. It became steeper still as he approached the coast. The trees, too, looked more stunted, and the shapes of some of them had been distorted as they attempted to resist the winter storms blowing in off the sea. As he looked over the stone wall into one field he saw what he thought might be a Bronze Age barrow – as, indeed, it was. At the top of the road Elijah's breath was taken away. The view was glorious. He was on a cliff top, looking across to cliffs on the opposite side of the bay. Down below was a glorious sandy beach, and Elijah hurried down to it.

The beach was deserted, the few holiday makers who had ventured this far along slow roads having left, and the local children now being under the gaze of Daniel, Elwyn and their colleagues. The tide was out, and Elijah could see dozens of outcrops of rock at the bottom of the cliffs on either side of the bay. He spent some time exploring the rock pools with their myriad forms of minuscule aquatic life. He knew that in the old days there had been a sizeable fishing industry based at Bethel beach, but those days were gone. A few boats were left, but they were mostly kept by locals for hobby purposes, except when the visitors were about. Then the lads would put to sea and bring back catches of mackerel for immediate sale on the shore.

Up by the road there were a few tank traps, survivors of the War. They had been put there in case Hitler made an assault on Britain from Eire. They had never been needed for that purpose, but they had become so much a part of the scenery that they would have been missed had they been removed. On a piece of land just above the beach there stood the lifeboat house. In the scrubby grass around it Elijah could see the purple flowers of what most knew as thrift, what some knew as sea pink, and what Elijah knew as *armeria maritima*. A slipway led from the front door onto the beach. The RNLI boat was manned by volunteers, and, apart from a couple of practices, it had been called out just once during the summer now past. That was when the Walters twins had found a large old tyre behind Derek Hart's garage, rolled it to the beach, clambered on it, and launched themselves into the water. The current had got the better of them, and had Constable Powell not been cycling by at the time, they might have been lost. PC Powell raised the alarm, and the volunteer crew came as fast as their bikes would carry them. They opened the boathouse door, pulled the boat down the slipway, launched it, and made the rescue without a hitch. The coxswain praised the men for their gallantry, and at the same time felt thoroughly humiliated, for his name was Eryl Walters, father of the twins, volunteer fireman and coxswain. That evening he gave the twins a piece of his mind.

'Have you forgotten last November 27th?'

They could hardly have forgotten it because Eryl spoke about it most days – and, indeed, it had been the talk of the district for weeks.

'What happened, then,' he asked them, and they replied almost in chorus: 'The *World Concord* broke in two in the Irish Sea.'

'How much did it weigh?'

'Twenty-two thousand tons.'

'How many attempts did the St David's lifeboat make to reach it?'

'Thirty-four.'

'Who else helped?'

'The Rosslare lifeboat.'

'How high were the waves?'

'Up to twenty feet.'

'How many lives were lost?'

'None.'

'So what do we learn from this?'

Silence.

'What we learn is that lifeboatmen are very brave, and they don't need to be messed about by scoundrels like you. Go to bed. And tomorrow you can take the tyre back to Mr Hart and tell him how sorry you are that you stole it.'

And off to bed they slunk.

Elijah returned to the road, turned left at the end of the beach and walked back up the hill to the Manse, passing on his left the road down to the village.

No sooner had he closed the door than the phone rang. He picked it up, and on the line was Jenkin Jones.

'Sad news today,' he said, 'dear old Mrs Ellen Roderick has passed on.'

'I'm very sorry to hear that,' said Elijah, who had, of course, never met the deceased, this being his first weekday at work. 'Can you tell me something about her?'

'Yes,' said Jenkin. 'She was ninety-eight. She'd been a member with us for eighty years, and was a very loyal supporter.'

'Where did she live?' asked Elijah.

'At Mayfield Farm' Jenkin replied.

'Did she live with anyone there whom I could visit?'

'Her husband died years ago, but her son lives with her. He's seventy two, and a widower. It'll be a big funeral.'

'Why do you say that?'

'Because she was very generous and popular, and very good at producing ministers. Her son is Roderick, Salem. His son, Roderick, is Roderick the Mission, and you were at College with his son, Roderick.' The last named had not yet received his label, but he soon would, to avoid confusion with the more senior members of his family, both of whom, to complicate matters further, were called John, as was he.

Now Elijah was getting the picture. This was indeed a prominent Congregational dynasty. Salem was one of the largest churches in the denomination. The exploits of Roderick the Mission were well known in many chapels, to which he had gone on furlough from the London Missionary Society with his talks and lantern slides. The more niggardly he expected his audiences to be, the more he heightened the accounts of his exploits so that they would be shamed into supporting one so heroic in the Lord's work. As for the Roderick of College days, he was pleasant enough, but so much of a duffer at Greek that the Principal and Professors had decided not to risk Hebrew with him; and he had that slightly overbearing manner which suggested to others that he regarded himself as cut out for great things. He had gathered a large collection of sentimental poems with which he punctuated his sermons, the remaining parts of which were so full of hot air that they could have launched a balloon.

Jenkin continued, 'The family wants you to fix things with Harries the Morgue at Newbridge Co-op. They have a grave space, and they suggest Friday at 3.00 if that suits you and Harries. I'll leave you to it, then.' And with that he was off the line.

So Elijah set to. Harries the Morgue was obsequious, as is the way with some of those of his profession – at least until you know them. And he was cooperative too – as well he might have been given his employer. Elijah confirmed the date and time with him and with Roderick, Salem, and invited the latter to say a few words. Inviting a Welsh minister to 'say a few words' is among the greatest pitfalls in Welsh religious life. They often find it quite impossible to be brief, especially if they belong to the old homiletic school in which Roderick, Salem, had been schooled. According to this tradition, 'You tell 'em what you're going to tell 'em; then you tell 'em; and then you tell 'em what you've told 'em.' But there

was no way in which Elijah could have avoided the risk. He next telephoned Roderick the Mission, who agreed to offer the 'long' prayer. That
left the Bible reading for young Roderick. He agreed to read, trying to
suppress the ungodly thought that if his great-grandmother had 'remembered' him suitably he might be able to complete the furnishing of his
Manse. Finally, Elijah telephoned Arnold Jackson at the *Sentinel*, and was
just in time to get an announcement of the death and funeral arrangements into that week's issue. Arnold was delighted – not that Mrs
Roderick had died, but because with such a big funeral to report he
would not have to pad out next week's paper, or print Letters to the
Editor with which he did not agree. All the arrangements made, Elijah
walked to Mayfield Farm to visit Roderick, Salem.

Funerals in rural Wales were events. People came from miles around.
Hetty always had to replenish her stock of black ties. And there was
always a big tea. They were competitive events, too, with one family
vying with another in respect of the number of ministers in attendance.
Constable Powell was always present, there being no pavements on the
narrow roads, and the Edwards Brothers' bus having been known to take
corners too sharply. 'Don't want any more deaths than the one in hand,'
PC Powell had said, dryly, on one occasion.

The service went well, though there were more people outside the
chapel than in: the turnout was enormous. For the first of many times
Elijah set eyes upon Harries the Morgue. As was the way with those of
his profession, he was in black from his top hat to his shoes, and his pallid features, deep-sunk eyes and multiple chins gave him a hang-dog look.
The coffin was removed from the hearse. The bearers were all Rodericks
from near and far, and none of them tripped as they solemnly processed
into the chapel.

Elijah conducted the service, and those appointed to take part did so.
Roderick, Salem, was as mellifluous and repetitive as ever; Roderick the
Mission thanked God for his grandmother's life and witness, and then
took God on a tour of the fields of the London Missionary Society;
Young Roderick read Psalm 23, spoiling it, in Elijah's opinion, by failing
to see that the verse about walking through the shadow of death and fearing no evil was the *fortissimo* verse in the entire psalm, and one not to be

spoken *pianissimo* just because the word 'death' was in it. Before the proceedings began, Jenkin Jones had come up to Elijah and said, 'It's the custom in these parts to invite any ministers present to say a few words if they'd like to.' This put pressure on Harries the Morgue's timetable, and on the ministers present. For it would look rude if one or more of them said nothing, and quite often they did not know the deceased very well. But Welsh ministers can usually be relied upon to overcome the latter inhibition. Elijah gave the invitation, and no fewer than twelve ministers said their few words.

Then Elijah and Harries the Morgue walked in front of the coffin and out to the freshly dug grave. The ministers and the members of the congregation followed. As they went between other graves, Harries the Morgue said, 'I always enjoy Bethel funerals.'

'Why's that?' asked Elijah, thinking that Harries's countenance was the most miserable he had ever seen.

'Because it's the best tea in the county,' said the undertaker. 'Nobody makes Welsh cakes like Mrs Rachel Morris.'

In the procession following the coffin were Jenkin Jones and Dai Cashbox. Said Dai to Jenkin, 'They're going to have a rough time in Madagascar next week.'

'Why's that?' enquired Jenkin.

'Because Roderick the Mission left Madagascar out of his prayer – the only mission field he forgot!'

By that time they had reached the grave, and Elijah conducted the burial service. Then they all went for tea, handing out cups of tea and plates to those who could not squeeze into the schoolroom. As the tea and cakes came his way, for the first time the pallid features of Harries the Morgue broke into a beatific smile.

4

The Reverend Elijah Morgan
Imbibes Culture and Finds a Hobby

Those who have the honour of being called to the pastorate of a Congregational church are not normally presented with a formal list of duties. The unwritten list is ample enough. It is universally expected – and what could be more natural? – that the minister will preach the gospel, administer the sacraments, conduct weddings and funerals, and visit the flock. But in Wales this is by no means all. In Wales the Congregational minister must love music.

There are local eisteddfodau in which the young – not to mention their parents – are locked in something approaching mortal combat. Before he had unpacked all his boxes, the Reverend Elijah Morgan received a visit from Mrs Blodwen Llewellyn, LRAM, organist. It appeared that the late Reverend Goronwy Rees had always supported the village eisteddfod; she felt sure that Mr Morgan would wish to do the same; and she would expect him in the Sunday School room the following Saturday at 9.30 sharp. With that she was off to put the finishing touches to her pupils, she said; and Elijah suddenly had a vision of those dog shows where pampered pets are given a final combing, or a touch of talcum power before they enter the ring.

Saturday came, and there was a discordant hubbub in the schoolroom. Little girls in their best frocks were repeating their lines and warming up their voices. Small boys, looking unusually tidy for a Saturday, were playing at conkers in the corner or fighting on the stage behind the drawn curtain. In the middle of the hall was the adjudicator's table, and in the middle of the table one of those brass bells which pierce the air when the knob on the top is struck.

At 9.28 the side door was flung open, and in swept the adjudicator, Madame Florence Matthias, LLAM, proprietor of the School of Music and Drama in town. Her appearance was somehow paradoxical. Her posture was excellent as befitted one trained at The London Academy of Music and Dramatic Art, but what hung on her skeleton was – how can one put it tactfully? – somewhat less disciplined. But all was hidden under billowing folds of colourful material. Her mauve velvet hat, which clashed with some of the colours in the rest of her ensemble, was a triumph of the milliner's art. With its very wide brim it would have been a great blessing in the desert, but it was strictly redundant for all practical purposes in the schoolroom. As her qualification and training suggested, Madame Matthias's speciality was speech and drama, but some forty years ago she had understudied the role of Hanna Glawari, Franz Lehár's *Merry Widow*, in Bournemouth – and that at a time when Mizzi Günther's creation of the role was still fondly remembered. On the strength of this she had incorporated music into her field of adjudication. Her adjudications were memorable for their visual imagery and almost complete lack of scientific underpinning: 'Sing through the chimney on top of your head,' she would warblingly command aspiring Hannas, her flailing arms protruding from her multi-layered sleeves; and this with entire disregard for anything resembling the findings of centuries of anatomical and physiological knowledge.

Mrs Blodwen Llewellyn swooped upon Elijah, who had been sitting in the back row in the seat nearest to the door, hoping for a speedy getaway. '*Do* come to the front,' she invited – well, it was more of a command, and her grip on his arm was vice-like.

So he sat in the front.

At 9.30 prompt the bell was struck, silence reigned, and the proceedings began. The secretary introduced Madame Matthias. This took nearly ten minutes, even though, as the secretary had said, the celebrity was one who needed no introduction. Then the contest began in earnest. Cherubic children sang through their adenoids with slightly off-key gusto. Small boys, after much practice, assumed an innocent expression and a defiant posture and, as quickly as they could, got rid of such verse as Alison Winn's 'Johnny's pockets':

Johnny collects
Buttons and rings
Bits of a watch,
Cog wheels and springs,
Half eaten sweets ...

'My eye,' mused Elijah. 'When I frisked the Jones Top Farm's grandson after a day trip to the seaside last Saturday, I found a beer mat, half a packet of cigarettes and one of those cartoon postcards that I am really very ashamed to have understood.'

And through it all, the parents. Parents glowing with pride. Parents fussing their offspring. Parents silently willing their young to knock spots off the competition and emerge victorious, whilst openly agreeing that the main thing was not the winning, but the opportunity to perform in front of a audience. Parents with wanly smiling mouths and eyes which were saying, 'Put the boot in, my darlin'.'

The Reverend Elijah reflected that parents were probably fighting their battles through their children the land over. Of course, the circumstances would differ – especially in England. There the *ars belli* would probably include horse riding and ballet. At least the village youngsters were not so likely to crack their skulls or dislocate their hips at an eisteddfod. No sooner had he registered the thought when a competitor named Richard Moses, who had been wandering lonely as a cloud, was dazzled by the stage lights, stumbled off the platform, and landed on his head at Elijah's feet. Things moved fast. The uniformed Mrs Rachel Morris, embodying the local St John Ambulance Brigade, rushed forward, a stretcher was brought, young Moses was carted off, and Madame Matthias rose, gave a speech which would have done justice to the dead of two World Wars, and demanded that the committee produce a special prize for courage in adversity, and that it be presented to Richard Moses.

Elijah Morgan, not being married, had no children of his own, and could therefore empathise with the parents' anxieties only from a distance. But the eisteddfod brought him anxieties of a special kind. For this was one of the few occasions in the year when Mrs Blodwen Llewellyn, LRAM and Miss Tilly Watkin, LTCL were in the same room at the same time. If St Cecilia had ever existed she would have been ashamed of them. Their plots and counterplots put those of Owain Glyndwr against the English into the shade. They were rivals in so many respects. Blodwen was married, Tilly was not, for Maldwyn had chosen Blodwen. Blodwen played for the Congregationalists, Tilly for the Baptists. Above all, Blodwen entered candidates for the examinations of the Associated Board of the Royal Schools of Music, Tilly for those of Trinity College, London. The examinations of both Boards were held on different days in the day school hall each year, and Blodwen lived just opposite. How her curtains twitched as she counted Tilly's entrants! How her wrath was aroused if she spotted an erstwhile pupil of hers who had defected to Tilly and Trinity. 'I should think your Polly will do very well with *them*,' she would say to the offending parent at the first opportunity.

Elijah could not judge her too harshly, however. Had he not felt grief – even anger – when the Rector 'creamed off' his brightest Sunday scholar for confirmation in the Parish Church? Nevertheless, he was still worried about Blodwen, for organists hold great power in their hands, and if her pupils did not achieve maximum success at the eisteddfod, he knew that the following day she would take it out on the congregation. A wronged organist has a whole battery of demonic ways of venting spleen. It is said that on one occasion Blodwen had played a different tune to each verse of a seven verse hymn. Another time she had transposed 'Cwm Rhondda' up a major third – and to have Welsh basses reduced to silence in that hymn of all hymns is as cruel as to throw a succulent bone for a dog whose legs are tied. But Blodwen's *pièce de résistance* was back in 1943. Tilly's pupils had completely outflanked hers at the eisteddfod on the Saturday, and on the Sunday, as a voluntary, she improvised a series of only very thinly disguised variations on the theme of 'There was I, waiting at the church ...'

But Congregational ministers in Wales do not only have to like the music and verse of children. They have to like Sankey Festivals, where the 'good old hymns' – most of them less than sixty years old – are lustily sung, and pathetic solos are tearfully rendered. The Reverend Elijah Morgan was expected to have a misty look in his eye as the Wagnerian spinster, Madame Myfanwy Price-Edwards wobbled her way through the tear-jerker, 'Where is my wandering boy tonight?' And he dared not smirk when Albert the Union, with great pathos, bawled his way through 'Tell Mother I'll be there' just before making a beeline for the pub. It almost came as a relief when Meirion came back from a visit to London with a copy of the *Billy Graham Song Book*, from which such sentimental offerings were almost entirely excluded. Meirion had treated himself to two nights in a bed and breakfast near White City stadium, so that he could hear the young American evangelist in person. He had been most impressed by Billy's 'message', and he returned home not only with the *Song Book*, but with a slogan ideally suited to launch his frequent judgemental utterances: 'The Bible says ...'

Where sacred music was concerned, Elijah learned early that he could not speak his whole mind in the pulpit without running a grave risk. On his third Sunday at Bethel he had dared to criticise Stainer's *Crucifixion* in a sermon. 'Its harmonies are banal, its lyrics sentimental,' he had said. At this even old Dewi Rowlands was aroused. 'Down boy,' he interjected, momentarily forgetting that he was in church and not at a sheep dog trial. Elijah desisted, but the deacons called an emergency meeting to discuss matters with him.

'The sooner you get those new-fangled College ideas out of your head, the better,' said Albert the Union. Other deacons joined in the chorus, and Elijah promised to display greater sensitivity in the future. He thought this would end the matter, but the deacons, with the understandable exception of Mrs Rachel Morris, got their own back. They rallied the menfolk, and during the service on the following Sunday they gave a spirited male voice rendering of Stainer's 'God so loved the world' – just to show him! – which grew progressively flatter as it went along.

Although Congregational ministers in Wales were expected to like music, their tastes, in this as in other things, must not be too catholic. Jazz and dance music were out. Their associations – smoke-filled cellars and dingy dance halls – were all wrong. Perhaps it was as well, therefore, that just as the churches did not produce full job specifications for their ministers, so the ministers were not bound to divulge every detail of their CVs. Were it otherwise, it would have emerged that whilst at the Theological College, Elijah Morgan had been reserve drummer of the

Saintly Stompers. This riotous ensemble met every week after sermon class and really let their hair down! The drums had come by a circuitous route from the Royal Marines. The trumpeter had been converted at a Billy Graham overflow meeting in Pontypridd, and had thereby been saved from a life of sin and busking outside the Odeon. The principal drummer worked out all his aggressions on the drums in one hour per week, and for the rest of the time canvassed for the pacifist Fellowship of Reconciliation.

While some of the budding preachers at the College idolised Leslie Weatherhead ('Vacuous psychological piffle glued together with homely anecdotes,' said the Calvinist Principal Morgan MacDonald), and the BD students bandied about the name of Rudolf Bultmann (whom they pretended to have read, knowing that few in the chapels would be any the wiser), Elijah Morgan almost broke the first Commandment over Gene Krupa. That man's hands! He pounded skins, cymbals and skulls so fast you couldn't see the drumsticks!

As for dance music, Elijah was always glad that he had not been born too late to hear Ambrose and Lew Stone, slick ambassadors of the imaginative arrangement and haunting melody. Sometimes, as he was dropping off to sleep he would have a vision of serried ranks of round-shouldered, pot-bellied saxophonists playing in that great ballroom in the sky. Once, as he was ruminating on his musical heroes in one of Principal MacDonald's lectures, he heard that good man mention the name of Ambrose, and blurted out, 'I do like his signature tune, "When day is done"!' 'No, Mr Morgan,' said the Principal as the rest of the class tittered, 'I am referring to Saint Ambrose, not Bert Ambrose, and you must get the distinction clear in your mind before you write your next essay.' Sure enough, the next essay was about Ambrose of Milan. But Elijah skilfully wove into his essay, without using quotation marks, seventeen of the titles recorded by Bert Ambrose, and he did it in such a way as to make intelligible prose concerning Ambrose of Milan. Three weeks later, as he was making his way to the dining hall, he saw Dr MacDonald approaching from the opposite direction. As they passed, the Principal said, 'I got all seventeen, and you got an A+ for ingenuity.'

Whereas the Baptist pastor Calvin Rowlands, Horeb, could, and usually did, quote the Puritans in every other sentence, Elijah had instant recall of lyrics from old standards of the kind of which it is said, 'They don't write them that way any more.' Such was his facility in this regard that on one occasion he nearly met his downfall. In unusually expansive mood, the deacons were congratulating him on his tactful handling of the affair of Angharad John's premature baby. In a way, Angharad was more premature than the baby, for the latter appeared six weeks before his mother's wedding. Elijah had been the soul of tact, and Angharad's mother had praised him to the skies to Dilys Jones, who told Jenkin, who told the deacons. With becoming modesty Elijah brushed aside the dia-conal effusions of praise, modestly murmuring, ''T'aint what you do, it's the way that you do it.' Then he called them swiftly to prayer.

Although there was more than enough room in the Manse for a drum kit – indeed for an entire band, Elijah could not afford one and, in any case, what would the neighbours have said? But he could, and did, afford a washboard and a number of thimbles. Often, after a particularly unruly deacons' meeting he would restore his soul by playing Humphrey Lyttel-ton's Parlophone recording of 'The Onions' on his gramophone. This he would accompany on his washboard. One day, thus occupied, he was so transported that he did not at first hear the doorbell ring. It persisted, and when the record ended he heard the bell and rushed down. There stood a breathless Megan Johnson. 'Mr Morgan, Mr Morgan,' she blustered in great excitement, 'I'm a granny!' Elijah made appropriate congratulatory noises and then noticed that Mrs Phillips was staring at his right hand. Elijah looked sheepishly down. She never guessed the reason. All she said was, 'Mr Morgan – *four* thimbles at once? We must find you a wife.'

The colour drained from Elijah's face. 'Goodnight,' he said, and closed the door quickly, feeling very threatened.

The next morning Elijah awoke in pensive mood. As if it were not enough that he should strive to live by the Ten Commandments and – which was even harder – meet the stringent moral standards by which his more pious deacons thought everyone else should live, he had also to balance those mutually contradictory moral injunctions for which most of us are indebted to our mothers.

He could see his mother now, standing over him, wagging her finger at him and saying, 'I'll teach you to go scrumping in neighbour Vaughan's orchard! "The Devil makes work for idle hands!" You will clean all our shoes for Sunday.' Shoe polishing being a forbidden occupation on the Sabbath itself, this meant that a slice of Saturday was ruined.

This memory was replaced by another. Elijah was now toiling over Pythagoras in his bedroom. It was a dark, gloomy night. His oil lamp flickered, making moving images on the wall which would have made even the ancient geometer query his principles. His mother's head came around the door: 'Have you not finished your homework yet? All this study is making you pale. Ease up, son, "All work and no play makes Jack a dull boy!"'

Thus was Elijah beset by true religion, by folk religion, and now by the deacons as well. He really did his best, and it was his very diligence which had brought him low. An unusually heavy toll of funerals, each requiring a more histrionic panegyric than its predecessor, and each followed by ham tea in which the widow sought, by culinary means, to outdo other widows by the provision of ever spicier pickles, to the distress of Elijah's digestive system – all of this began to tell.

As if the funerals were not enough, there were Elijah's attempts to contain the Youth Club during its leader's absence on a course; and there were those endless discussions with the social worker about whether the Club could reasonably be deemed recuperative in the case of a young man who had been diagnosed as mentally exhausted and plied with enormous quantities of medication. In Elijah's opinion – and experience – ten minutes with the chapel Youth Club would bring the strongest to breaking-point.

On top of all this, during the severe weather in early December, when even the waterfall was frozen, numerous members of the congregation – not only those who had the excuse of being frail and elderly – had, with no thought for their minister's well-being, fallen sick. The more remote their farms, the more snow-blocked their drives, the more seriously ill they were. In urgent cases Elijah had hitched lifts on the Council snow plough in order to reach them. This mode of transport so shook him up that he thought his frozen bones must snap.

Small wonder that the Reverend Elijah Morgan felt jaded. He wrestled with his problem. He was one of the most conscientious of ministers. He must be a good steward of his time. He must not work himself into the ground. His mother's homely adages floated back into his mind. So did Professor Llewellyn-Jones's lectures on Aristotle's mean. But neither the learned Professor nor the Greek sage had had deacons to contend with.

Then came a flash of inspiration: he must take up a hobby. Get some perspective on it all. But what should he do? There was an amateur dramatic society in the village. Every year they put on a show in the day school hall. But this was ruled out on a number of counts. In the first place, Elijah well remembered the fate of the minister-cum-amateur-thespian, the Reverend Arthur Tudor, back in his home town. This worthy had the voice and bearing of an ac-*tor*. Whereas the great eighteenth-century actor, David Garrick, longed to be able to say 'Ohhh!!!' like the evangelist George Whitefield, Arthur Tudor could do it – and then some! He was tall and burly, his voice was deep, his enunciation perfect, his pulpit gestures over the top, his pauses for profile magnificent. He was the ideal Abanazer for the Beulah Baptists' production of *Aladdin*. (It will be remembered that among the Baptists there are greater degrees of godliness – and worldliness – than among the members any other Christian denomination; and from the fact that the Reverend Calvin Rowlands's doctrinal scruples would not permit him to attend Elijah's ordination we should not conclude that all Baptists would have behaved similarly. Arthur Tudor could ham it up with the best – or the worst – of them.) So it was. He was cast as Abanazer; and for ever afterwards, when giving vent to one of his dramatic pulpit descriptions of the pains of hell, little boys would interject, 'Where's the magic smoke?' or 'Look out, the Good Fairy's behind you!' To Elijah all of this was a considerable dissuasive.

There were other considerations too. The amateur dramatic society had something of a reputation for match-making, and Elijah knew that if he went there he would find himself amongst a number of young ladies whose mothers thought of him as the ideal son-in-law. He would not wish to be in a position where he was obliged to kiss any of them – even for the sake of art, and certainly not for any other reason.

And then, as so often, it all came back to the deacons. To some of them – especially to Meirion Hughes – the theatre was a sink of iniquity, and Meirion was quite unable to get his mind around the fact that the number of village maidens whose fall was directly connected with the activities of the local thespians was statistically insignificant. It was said that when Albert the Union and his wife Ada came back from holiday in Blackpool one year and let slip that they had seen Jimmy James on stage – 'That lion in the shoebox,' said Albert, tears of mirth rolling down his cheeks at the remembrance of it – Meirion refused to speak to them for a month.

Acting was definitely out. How about something more suited to Bethel's rural surroundings? Shooting, perhaps? Elijah had often fancied himself behind a gun – especially during some of the more boisterous deacons' meetings. But was this a worthy sport for a pacifist? For pacifist he was, though he did not trumpet the fact. Of course, one could plead gun practice for reasons of self defence, but the only occasion of violence in the village's corporate memory was the drunken brawl between Roberts the milk and Edwards the meat, and that was settled not with a shoot-out, but by their both simultaneously keeling over. Most people thought that shooting was all right for the Rector, but for a Nonconformist minister to take it up – that might betoken Establishment pretensions, and that would never do.

How about tennis? It was not yet the season for it, but Elijah could look forward to longer days and happy hours on the excellent courts behind the day school. He became quite excited at the prospect, but then remembered that those same young ladies who played romantic leads in the winter graced the tennis courts in the summer; so tennis was ruled out.

As for other games, the local cricket team persisted in desecrating the Sabbath, while the footballers were given to Bacchanalian revels in victory and to sorrow-drowning binges in defeat. They would curse the ball, the opponents, the referee, inadequate team-mates and even, on occasion, the Almighty himself. Another piece of his mother's worldly wisdom came floating back to Elijah: 'A man is judged by the company he keeps.' The soccer team would have to do without him.

Elijah had by now exhausted all the possibilities he could think of, and there the matter rested for a while. In any case, he had other things to think of. Mrs Marshall, Hendre, had been blessed with triplets, and he must make for the nursing home in town to congratulate her on behalf of the church, bestow flowers upon her, and say a prayer. So off he went on the bus to town. The triplets admired, the prayer said, Elijah left and made his way back to the bus stop. He consulted the timetable and found that he had twenty minutes to kill.

Opposite the bus stop was the newsagent's. Elijah crossed over and began aimlessly to twirl the stands. He could hardly reach the magazines at the top, but he could see, from a very rapid glance, that these were illustrated by heavenly bodies – and not of the kind that Denys the Pseudo-Areopagite was always going on about. Adjusting his gaze to a more comfortable level, Elijah saw magazines on pop music, motor cars and gardening. There was the inevitable pile of *Exchange and Mart*, and there, almost hidden by *The Lady* was *The Airgunner*. Elijah cast a furtive glance over his right shoulder and over his left, and then moved fast – there might be deacons about. He picked up the evening paper, slipped *The Airgunner* inside it, went to the counter and paid for both, and left the shop hurriedly as the bus hove into view.

Back at the Manse he cast the newspaper aside and read his magazine avidly. There was a lot to be said for target shooting, he thought. It trained the eye. Nothing got killed. None of the daughters of the pastorate was remotely interested in it. And the deacons had never been heard to condemn it. At the back of *The Airgunner* were some classified advertisments and some club listings. Providence! There was a club in the next town but two. 'Meetings on Tuesdays at 7.30 p.m. Newcomers welcome.' Providence again! Only last week the deacons had decided to move the Prayer meeting from Tuesdays to Wednesdays. Elijah knew where he would be next Tuesday!

And there he was, in his most casual clothes. Agricultural workers, quarrymen, a few youths, some chewing gum – they all eyed the newcomer with much interest, and they welcomed him warmly. 'Of course,' said stocky Mike Benson the secretary, 'to become a regular member you have to submit two character references. But you can have a try-out tonight to see if you like it.'

They gave Elijah some basic instruction, and then he found himself on the floor, facing the targets which seemed very small and far away. He did surprisingly well. He got the highest score of the evening, and was the only man in that club who had ever allowed himself to be treated to a celebratory lemonade. As for references – Elijah knew exactly on whom to call. There was the Reverend Luther Jones who, unknown to his deacons, was chaplain and snooker champion at the local territorials; and there was the Reverend Christmas Powell who had recently, with equal ecclesiastical discretion, earned himself a silver cup for being darts champion in a certain hostelry – the very one which was the object of his senior deacon's numerous petitions to the Council to have it closed down.

Elijah had found a hobby! That night he dreamed happily. A series of targets passed before his eyes, and in the centre of each was not a bull's eye, but a familiar face. 'Every one a deacon,' he chuckled in his sleep. And when he woke up next morning an impish – even a slightly wicked – grin was still playing about his lips.

5

The Reverend Elijah Morgan
Saves the Boiler

It was another crisp December morning. A weak sun was doing its best
to vanquish a heavy frost. A stiff breeze was contriving to reduce the
temperature still further. Elijah Morgan was in his study, the sash windows of which were rumbling against the breeze, and letting a good deal
of it in. Elijah was seated at his desk, smothered by a huge, thick, pullover
knitted lovingly by his grandmother as an ordination present. He was
tapping out a sermon on his Corona typewriter – an ordination present
from his parents. By his side burned a paraffin fire, an ordination present
from his agnostic brother, Caleb, given, said Caleb 'to remind you of the
flames of hell'.

Just as he was getting to the punchline of his sermon, Elijah noticed
Jenkin Jones, Top Farm, coming up the garden path. He looked utterly
downcast. 'Oh dear,' sighed Elijah, 'not another funeral!'

He went to the door and let Jenkin in. 'Has somebody died?' he asked.

'No, no, much worse than that,' replied Jenkin. What could it be?
Jenkin was clearly in shock. 'I've just had Mrs Dai Cashbox on the phone,'
he said, 'and she says that Dai has been up all night praying.'

'Is that so disastrous?' enquired Elijah, remembering that the saints of
old would sometimes devote many hours to prayer – and fasting too.

'Of course it is,' blustered Jenkin. 'He only does that when there's a
financial calamity.'

'So what has caused the calamity?' asked Elijah.

'Bethel's boiler has burst,' declared Jenkin, with difficulty restraining
himself from adding further words to what was already a sufficiently allit-
erative sentence.

'Oh, I'm so sorry,' said Elijah, in exactly the same tones he would have used if somebody had died; and as he said it he wondered, irrelevantly, why, since boilers were the pampered idols of Nonconformist chapels, nobody had thought of including a service for a defunct boiler in the *Manual for Ministers* which Congregational ministers were at liberty (though not, of course, required) to use.

Elijah could see from Jenkin's distress that extreme pastoral tact was called for. He therefore phrased an implicitly optimistic question which assumed that the boiler was repairable: 'How long do you think it will take to put it right?'

'About a day,' said Jenkin. Elijah inwardly sighed with relief. He would not have to read the last rites over the boiler – yet. Then the question demanding even more pastoral sensitivity: 'Do you think we shall have to pay as much as the Baptists did when their boiler gave out last year?' Elijah knew that everybody knew that the Baptists had been rooked by a Presbyterian plumber, and he thought that his question would assist Jenkin to make the adjustment of perspective – provided that Bethel's boiler repair would cost less than £12.00.

'Ben U-bend has told Dai Cashbox that it'll cost £10.00, and Dai says we shall need a special event to raise the money.' It is not necessary to explain that Jenkin used the name by which the local plumber and heating engineer was universally known – well, known to all in the valley, many of whose inhabitants would have been hard put to remember what his real surname was.

'Give me some time to think about this,' said Elijah. 'I'll get back to you tomorrow morning.' And with that Jenkin went back to his farm, his sad tidings conveyed.

Elijah had little time to reflect on the matter immediately. He had to finish his sermon and then go to town. This meant catching one of the infrequent buses from the village stop. He must be quick. His sermon was about our obligation to care for the less fortunate, and the boiler gave him the final illustration he needed. Having great faith that members of the congregation would open their purses rather than shiver all through the service next Sunday, Elijah typed, 'How blest we are to have such a cosy chapel as this, with our newly mended boiler to keep us all warm.' He then typed [PAUSE] in brackets. This was partly for effect, and partly because whenever the moral of the sermon was in the offing Albert the Union would catch a whiff of coke fumes and burst into almost uncontrollable coughing, thereby ruining Elijah's climax. 'Let us think, then,' continued Elijah, 'of all those less fortunate than ourselves, and let us do our best to help them.' As he typed this last sentence he could imagine Meirion Hughes, his fundamentalist deacon, thinking, 'bland humanism – where's the blood of the Lamb?' But Elijah had to get to the bus stop, and so the conclusion stood.

Eventually the bus reached town. There was the ruined castle, beyond it the cattle market and the town centre. It seemed that nearly every street had a church on it – all the main denominations were present, as well as a number of gospel halls, the Salvation Army citadel, and even the meeting halls of the Christadelphians and the Jehovah's Witnesses. Some of the grandest chapels had been built by businessmen or factory owners who wished at one and the same time to glorify God and to outdo their business rivals who belonged to other traditions. There was the Regal Cinema, whose name belied its appearance, and there were even more pubs than churches. On the opposite side of town was the hospital, and this was Elijah Morgan's primary target.

Old Mrs Bowen had 'gone in with her legs', as Elijah was reliably informed, and his task was to minister pastoral care to her. It was his first hospital visit, and he felt just a little apprehensive. He did not much care for hospitals, his one encounter with which so far had been in connection with the removal of his appendix at the age of twelve. His nurse had been one of the old school, and everything she said: 'It won't hurt,' 'You'll enjoy this meal,' and 'We're feeling much better today, aren't we?' turned out to be untrue. As he went through the big doors of the hospital his mood was, not surprisingly, sceptical.

The professor of Pastoral Theology at the Theological College was the Reverend Geraint Jenkins. He had been a chaplain to the RAF during the war. When he enlisted for war service he was, by all accounts, just a run-of-the-mill pastor mouthing one or other of the five or six platitudes to which his kind are given whenever pastoral emergency strikes. But the war, if it did not increase his pastoral sensitivity, had certainly given him a new language. On demobilisation he had returned to his pastorate and his deacons had been astounded to be addressed as 'Old sport' – even 'Old thing'. The arrangers of the annual bazaar were more than a little surprised to hear their efforts described in votes of thanks as 'Bang on! Tickety-boo!' The churches were spared when he was called to the Chair of Pastoral Theology, a discipline not infrequently the refuge of the half crazed.

The previous holder of the Chair had been Professor Geraint Parry, a gracious scholar, hymn writer and liturgiologist, author of many books and a number of technical papers on the placing of the epiclesis in the communion service. Even after years of his patient instruction Congregational ordinands left his loving presence without being altogether clear what the epiclesis was, or where to put it. The new professor could not have been a greater contrast. He was the Joe Blunt of pastoral care. Not for him the non-directive approach of that young American, Carl Rogers. When one day a distraught church member had wailed, 'Why has all this happened to me?' Jenkins had abruptly replied, 'Because you're a rotten old sinner!' It would not be strictly accurate to say that Jenkins had given no guidance to the ordinands concerning hospital visitation. It is just that his guidance, 'Call 'em all Matron. Get 'em eatin' out of your hand, and Bob's your uncle! Tickety boo!' was not the most practical or exhaustive. All of which increased Elijah's apprehensiveness as he tried to remain upright on the polished floor, and as his nostrils became acclimatised to that mixed carbolic-ammonia smell.

He read the signs, and turned in the direction of the female wards. No sooner had he gone a few steps than from behind came the peremptory question, 'And where do you think you're going? Visiting hours are from three until five.' The accent was unmistakably Irish. He turned and saw a tall, erect nurse with iron grey hair in a dark blue uniform. She was of military bearing but, so far at least, had shown no familiarity with Professor Jenkins's military slang.

'Good afternoon, Matron,' said Elijah. 'I am the Reverend Elijah Morgan of Bethel Congregational Church, and I understand that as a minister of religion I am not tied to visiting hours.'

'My name is Sister O'Shaughnessy,' she replied, icily, 'and I am not blind. Where is your clerical collar? How do I know that you are not an imposter?'

Elijah's thoughts were in a whirl as he wondered how best to respond. Was this the occasion for a lecture on the theology of ministerial dress and how, since Congregational ministers do not regard themselves as members of a priestly caste they do not feel the necessity of wearing a Roman collar (unless they belong to that minority who try to ape the Anglicans)? Such an approach might only make matters worse, especially if, as was statistically likely, Irish Sister O'Shaugnessy was a Roman Catholic. Some more ecumenical approach would have to be found. Should he remind her of the famous words of the distinguished London Congregational minister, R. F. Horton? – words so famous that they found their way into the Logic textbook as a prime example of ambiguity: 'I will wear nothing to distinguish me from my fellow church members.' But as soon as he thought of it he realised that Sister O'Shaugnessy was in no mood to be teased about the niceties of ambiguous discourse, and that even if she had the patience to understand the point, which was doubtful, it was most unlikely that she had a sufficient sense of humour really to appreciate it. So he did the most practical thing. He reached into his pocket and pulled out one of his brand new visiting cards, the bill for which had been paid for by Dai Cashbox just before the boiler burst. It proudly proclaimed:

> **Bethel Congregational Church**
>
> **The Reverend Elijah Morgan, B.A., B.D.**
> **The Manse, Bethel**
>
> **Telephone 167**

Sister O'Shaugnessy read the card. She supposed it was genuine enough – at least as genuine as his ministerial orders were, which might not be saying much. Then she said,

'Go on your way, but don't get in the way. And make sure you're out of here by the time I knock off at 10.00 p.m.'

Getting in the way was the last thing Elijah wished to do. On the contrary, the sooner he could get out, the better he would be pleased. It would certainly not take him eight hours to make his call upon old Mrs Bowen. So off he went until he came to the ward where she was. She was so pleased to see him. For one who had spent her life on a remote farm her interrogation skills were honed to perfection. Elijah had gone there expecting to supply godly comfort and gospel reassurances, but in ten minutes flat she had extracted his life story from him. She knew more about him than anyone else at Bethel, and so had acquired a bolt of material suitable for embroidery on her return to Bethel – embroidery such as only the ladies of the Bethel Sewing Circle could accomplish.

Elijah wished Mrs Bowen well, greeted other patients as he passed by their beds, and found his way out of the hospital. His plan now was to find a café, and this he did. While waiting for his pot of tea, his pork pie and his Welsh cakes, he reflected upon what the evening had in store for him. For as well as his hospital visit it was his intention, partly out of denominational loyalty and partly out of utter curiosity to attend the evening lecture to be given by the Reverend Iorwerth Lewis, DD, of Ebenezer Congregational Church on 'The relevance of Denys the Pseudo-Areopagite's *Celestial Harmony* to Welsh Nonconformity'. What would the learned speaker have to say? How on earth – or rather, perhaps, by what heavenly intuitions – would he be able to show that Denys's nine orders of angels had much to do with the Bethel members?

In the event, Elijah never had his questions answered. Between the café and Ebenezer was the Rose and Crown, an old coaching inn with real oak beams, not brewers' mock Tudor. On the pavement outside was a sandwich-board proclaiming:

250th Anniversary of the Rose and Crown
Celebration Quiz Tonight
Entry Free
First prize £10   Second Price £5   Third prize £3

Elijah read the notice carefully and began to wrestle with his conscience. He had never been in a pub in his life. He had signed the temperance pledge as a youth. He truly believed that alcohol was a drug of addiction which ruined the lives of many individuals and families. But Bethel's boiler had burst. The only people in town who knew him were Sister O'Shaugnessy who was at work until 10.00 p.m., old Mrs Bowen who was in bed, and the Reverend Dr Iorwerth Lewis who would soon have his hands full with heavenly transports. It would be safe enough. And if he won, what a kindness it would be to relieve Dai Cashbox of a further sleepless night of ardent prayer. On balance the thing to do was to go in, enter the competition and do the best he could, secretly, for Bethel.

So in he went. The beams were low, the room was smoke-laden, the tables were set out with pencils and paper for the competitors. Elijah sat at a table. Mine host was the quizmaster. He was a jolly fellow whose appearance suggested that he enjoyed the profits in more ways than one. He called everyone to order. He explained that there would be a hundred questions, and that the range of topics would be wide. So the quiz began.

Some of the questions had to do with films, and you might have thought that one whose upbringing had excluded him from the cinema would have had great difficulty with these. But Elijah had had a paper round, and his deliveries could be up to forty-five minutes late on the morning when *Picturegoer* came out. He could recognise the stars; he knew the plots. So a question like, 'Who made her film debut in the 1944 film, *To Have and Have Not?*' was child's play – Lauren Bacall. Elijah even knew that she was born Betty Jane Perske in New York on 16 September 1924. But the Rose and Crown did not require that depth of knowledge.

There were questions on the Bible – well, Christmas was approaching. Elijah thought he might stand a good chance with these, but his heart sank when he heard the first one, 'What were the names of the three wise men who came to visit the infant Jesus?' This question revived memories of his New Testament professor, the Reverend Francis Algernon Gervase Ash who, even without those initials and that surname might, from the state of his clothes have earned the nickname Fag Ash. He was an enigma. He was a Jekyll and Hyde. On Sundays he was the beloved preacher, always welcome at anniversary services. He had four or five sermons that he took from place to place and used many times – these were known in the ministerial trade as 'travelling mercies'. To the congregations they were like

familiar old slippers. But the way he put them over! Nobody could cry in
the pulpit as frequently or as profusely as he – and crying, as everybody
agreed, was a primary mark of a particularly fine preacher. But on week-
days he was transmogrified into the wizened, cynical philologist and
textual critic. Insofar as there is any truth in the allegation that the point
of theological colleges is to knock the faith out of their clients, he was the
one at the Congregational College who did the demolition job. Many a
Bible-believing student became quite disorientated by Fag Ash's scepti-
cism. He didn't think that Jesus uttered the missionary command at the end
of Matthew's Gospel; he followed Goodspeed in doubting whether Paul
wrote Ephesians; and as for the three wise men, he wasn't sure whether
they ever existed, but if they did, the New Testament was silent as to their
number (though not as to their gifts); and as for their names, these were
unbiblical and were first bestowed upon them in the sixth century.

Elijah thought, 'Blow Fag Ash,' and wrote down Caspar, Melchior and
Balthasar.

There were questions on sport. Elijah did not know much about Grand
National winners, because such events were associated with that other
vice, gambling. And he had hardly ever heard of Women's Lacrosse, never
mind the names of any who played it. (He was not at all surprised when,
at the end of the quiz, mine host acknowledged that the quiz had been
devised by one Miranda Flowerdew-Symons of Henley-on-Thames). But
Elijah did know about football, and he put down the names of Tom
Finney, Nat Lofthouse and Tommy Lawton when the occasion arose.

One question was on radio programmes, and here he did really well.
His crystal set had entertained him for many hours as a boy, and he knew
that 'Can I do you now, Sir?' was Mrs Mopp of ITMA's phrase; that
Flying Officer Kite was a character in *Waterlogged Spa*; that Sam Costa
used to say, 'Good morning, Sir, was there something?' in *Much Binding in
the Marsh*; and that Whipit Quick the Cat Burglar was a character in
Charlie Chester's *Stand Easy*.

But, as we might expect from what we know of him, Elijah surpassed
all other competitors on the questions concerning popular music. He even
knew that the odd band leader out among Troise and his Mandoliers,
Don Porto and his Novelty Accordions, Rossini and his Accordions and

Primo Scala and his Accordian Band, was Troise. For Troise was Pasquale Troise from Naples (though his singer, 'Don Carlos' was actually Christopher Thomas Birrell O'Malley from – yes – Edinburgh!); the other three were aliases of Harry Bidgood from London.

The hundred questions asked, mine host the quizmaster asked every competitor to ensure that his or her name was on the answer papers (Elijah wrote simply 'Elijah Morgan'), and the papers were exchanged with a neighbour, and marked as the answers were given out. The tension in the air would have caused even Denys the Pseudo-Areopagite's angels to quiver a little with excitement. And then the result was announced.

In the tones employed by those introducing boxers in the ring, mine host said 'The Third Prize of £3 goes to Jack Collins,' and up went Jack to claim it. 'The Second Prize of £5 goes to Mrs June Collier,' and up she went to collect it. Elijah's mouth went dry – which was a pity because there was so little around that he felt morally able to drink. 'The First Prize of £10 goes to Elijah Morgan.' He could hardly believe it! Up went Elijah, received his congratulations and his crisp ten pound note, looked at his watch, and dashed out to catch the last bus home.

By the time he got to the Manse it was 10.45, but kindness prompted him to pick up the telephone and call Dai Cashbox. Mrs Betty Pugh answered. 'Dai was so worried about the boiler,' she said, 'that he went upstairs at nine to pray, and he'll be there all night again.' Elijah was quite moved by this example of persistence in emergency prayer. 'Go to him,' he said to Betty, choosing his words very carefully, 'and tell him that I have a donation which will cover the cost of repairing the boiler.' Betty went, and Dai had his best night's sleep for many a week.

The following morning, Thursday, Elijah took the £10 to Dai, and Ben U-bend was summoned. The work was done on the Friday, and the congregations – morning and night – were very comfortable on the Sunday.

Of course, everybody wanted to know where the money had come from, but Elijah's lips were sealed. Then it happened!

Out came the *Sentinel* the following Wednesday with a banner headline, MINISTER WINS PUB PRIZE! The cat was out of the bag – and the deacons were due to forgather that night! But how had the news leaked out? Elijah was sure that only three people in town knew him, and none of them was in the Rose and Crown. He later discovered that the Rose and Crown was the favourite watering hole of Brian 'Boozey' Bevan, whose name was on the news report. He was the *Sentinel*'s chief reporter and resident atheist. He loved nothing more than writing the obituaries of Christians – 'Another one bit the dust' he would say to himself as he carefully listed all the mourners. He had been in the pub on the night of the quiz; he had heard Elijah announced as the winner, and from a glance at the telephone book had discovered only one Elijah Morgan. It was a simple deduction.

The deacons forgathered.

'It's an utter disgrace!' expostulated Meirion Hughes as soon as the opening prayer was over. 'Going into a pub! Taking the devil's money!'

'But,' said Mrs Rachel Morris, 'You were so pleased to be warm in chapel on Sunday. Perhaps if we don't use the boiler for the next few Sundays until we've collected £10 in other ways, you'll be happy.'

'That's not the point,' says Meirion sulkily, thinking that he would not be at all happy to sit in a chapel resembling a freeze-box.

Dai Cashbox, feeling great relief about the knees now that the praying had ceased, spoke with the voice of sweet reason: 'But isn't it better to get money away from the brewers by fair means than letting them keep it and ruin more young lives?'

'If you're going to live by the Book you must die by it,' declared Elwyn Roberts the radical school teacher, turning the heat upon Meirion once more; 'and what about the verse in 1 Timothy 5:23, "use a little wine for thy stomach's sake..."?'

Meirion was silent. So was Albert the Union, though for different reasons – for did not a fair portion of his pension money flow in the direction of the brewer's coffers? And Albert was no hypocrite.

Then Elwyn the radical, using his authoritative school-prize-day voice, delivered his verdict: 'I think we should congratulate our minister on his ingenuity and his knowledge.'

And the church secretary, Jenkin Jones, declared in one of his rare biblically illustrated utterances, 'Mr Morgan was a veritable Daniel in a den of lions. And the Lord brought him out unscathed – and with ten quid too. Well done, lad! Next business.'

6

The Reverend Elijah Morgan
Enjoys the Festive Season

The deacons forgathered. It was to be their last meeting before Christmas.

'Let's keep it short,' said Albert the Union, whose liquid festivities always took longer around Christmas time, and he was anxious to give due place to things secular as well as sacred.

'The Lord's work is not to be rushed,' said Meirion, piously.

'Let us pray,' said Elijah, the call to prayer being an infallible way of halting diaconal banter.

There were no apologies. Jenkin Jones read the Minutes of the last meeting. As ever they were brief to the point of being curt. But Jenkin knew that the less he wrote, the less there would be to argue about. The Minutes accepted as a true record, Dai Cashbox then gave his customary interim financial report in his customary phrase, 'All's OK.' After that they confirmed the forthcoming seasonal events and activities, and then Elijah asked, 'Is there any other business?'

On numerous occasions in the past this apparently innocuous query had had fateful consequences. Any other business had been known to occupy the worthy deacons until after midnight. When Albert the Union was feeling particularly mischievous (or out of beer money) he would say, 'Let's have a whist drive,' knowing that the suggestion would bring Meirion close to apoplexy, and launch a lengthy argy-bargy on the subject of gambling in general and in the Lord's house in particular. At the following meeting Meirion would retaliate by saying, 'Let's have a week of revival meetings', even though he knew that everyone in the village had some sort of link to a church – except the genial humanist, Professor Gareth Reynolds who, as far as Meirion was concerned, was utterly beyond redemption.

On this occasion it was Jenkin Jones who spoke, and what he said had nothing to do with gambling or revivals.

'What Bethel needs is a second-hand tin tabernacle,' he said, 'and I know where there is one.'

This declaration, coming out of the blue as it did, provoked a silence seldom experienced at the deacons meeting.

'Why?' asked Elwyn Roberts.

'Because,' said Jenkin, 'our schoolroom is too small. When we have even an ordinary funeral we can't get them all in. Since Mr Morgan's been with us the Youth Club has grown and they need more space. There's never enough room at the Harvest Supper. And we could be a service to the village, because there's no village hall. And the Baptists won't have thought of that.'

He uttered the last sentence in tones suggesting that this was the clinching argument. Jenkin was astute, and knew how to appeal to denominational prejudice in a good cause.

All but one of the deacons thought of possible uses for a tin tabernacle but, mercifully, they did not speak their ideas aloud.

Jenkin could envisage an annual flower show.

Elwyn thought it would be possible to form a badminton club.

Albert the Union thought it would be an ideal venue for whist and possibly even for bingo.

Meirion thought that a branch of the Band of Hope could be established.

Mrs Rachel Morris thought that it would really show the Anglicans if the Women's Institute held its weekly sale of homemade cakes and jam there.

But Dai Cashbox was squirming in his seat. There were many points to settle before uses of the tin tabernacle could be contemplated, and most of them had to do with money.

'Where is this tin tabernacle and how much would it cost?' he asked.

'It's not far from Bridgend,' Jenkin replied. 'I saw the advert in the *Echo*. They want £100 for it, with the buyer to pay the cost of travel.'

'Who are "they"?' asked Albert.

This was the question Jenkin had dreaded. He braced himself and said,

'They are Roman Catholics and they're moving out of the tabernacle into their new church building.' There! The truth was out! Jenkin looked anxiously in the direction of Meirion.

'I don't much care for giving money to Roman Catholics,' Meirion said, as expected. 'And when I think what ceremonies have taken place in it I ...'

At this point Elwyn chipped in. 'You could always exorcise the tabernacle,' he quipped.

'That would be playing the Catholics at their own game,' said Meirion dolefully, having mistakenly taken Elwyn seriously. 'But,' he thought to himself, 'it *would* be good to have a Band of Hope.'

'What I don't understand,' said Elwyn, 'is how we would get the tabernacle here.'

Elwyn was expert in all matters pertaining to music and drama, and inexpert where buildings were concerned.

'There's no problem about that,' said Jenkin. 'These tabernacles come to bits. They have a wooden frame clad on the outside with corrugated iron, and with matchboard walls inside. You can paint them whatever colour you like. All we'd have to do would be to prepare the base for it, and put it up when it arrived.'

'That's not all we'd have to do,' said Dai Cashbox; 'we'd have to pay for it and for its carriage.'

'I have a suggestion about that,' said Elijah. 'But first, is there any more information you can give us, Mr Jones, about this particular tin tabernacle?'

'Yes,' said Elwyn. 'It has a small porch; five windows along each aside; and a back door on the right which leads into a storeroom.'

'Do you know who made it?' asked Albert the Union, who was quite well up in all things industrial and mechanical.

'Boulton and Paul of Norwich,' came the reply.

'The best in the business,' said Albert. 'They used to make railway wagons, and in 1925 they perfected the car in which Donald Campbell broke the land speed record by going at 150.87 miles per hour. Then they got into aircraft ...'

Elijah never ceased to be amazed at the miscellaneous information that his deacons had acquired over the years. But he could see that Albert was only just warming up, so he interjected, 'I think we'll all agree that the tin tabernacle came from an excellent company. Now, any further questions apart from the question how will we pay for it?'

'Yes,' said Rachel Morris, 'How will we get it here?'

'Well', said Jenkin, 'it will come by rail to Newbridge, and we'll have to find some way of bringing it the last seven miles.'

'Mollie will bring it,' said Albert the Union.

'Excellent job,' said Jenkin, while Elijah wondered who this muscular Mollie might be.

'Mollie?' he inquired.

'You come around to my place tomorrow,' said Albert, 'and you can meet her.' The others smiled knowingly, but said nothing.

'So, then,' said Elijah, 'we now come to costs.'

'About time,' muttered Dai Cashbox.

'I propose,' Elijah continued, 'that we all work hard and have a Grand Concert at the end of January so as to raise money for the tin tabernacle. We must tell everybody what the money is for, and let them know what a great asset the tin tabernacle will be to the community.'

'But however good the Grand Concert is,' moaned Dai, 'we'll never make £100. And then there's the cost of transport.'

'We must do our very best,' replied Elijah, 'and I believe it will all work out well in the end because Mr Jenkin Jones has heard a whisper.'

From past experience the deacons knew that only good could come when Jenkin had 'heard a whisper'. From past experience, too, they knew better than to ask him precisely what had been whispered. 'Jenkin always keeps his cards close to his chest; but he always knows when to play an ace,' mused Meirion, wondering how such an ungodly analogy had drifted into his mind.

They then got down to practicalities. Jenkin said that he and the men would see to the base for the tabernacle – there was plenty of land behind the chapel. Dai Cashbox forced himself to say that he would send the Roman Catholics £20 from chapel funds to reserve the tabernacle until they had the base ready and could collect it when the weather improved after Christmas. He could not deny that they had recently done better than expected at the Harvest sale of produce. Elwyn said that he would gather talent for the Grand Concert. Rachel Morris said she would be in charge of the refreshments. And even Meirion said he would serve as stage manager – that would at least get him out of actually performing in what he feared might be a thoroughly secular set of turns.

After the closing prayer they all set off for home. Elijah did not think he had seen them so animated before. As he left the hall Albert the Union turned and said to Elijah, 'Don't forget. Come around tomorrow and I'll introduce you to Mollie.'

The next morning Elijah set off to see who this Mollie was. Ada answered the door and invited him in. The house was clean and comfortable. A few pieces of older furniture – heirlooms from previous generations, Elijah thought, were accompanied by wartime utility items. They had a Welsh dresser, and Ada had discreetly removed Albert's pint pot which usually occupied a corner of it.

At that moment Albert came in. He was in his overalls, and there was a trace of smut across his brow.

'Good! You've got here,' he said to Elijah. 'Come out and meet Mollie.'

At the back of the house was a small kitchen garden, and beyond that were two adjoining buildings. The smaller of these Albert had converted into a workshop, and he proudly showed Elijah his neatly arranged tools, his lathe, and numerous other gadgets with which he whiled away his time. The larger building had once been stables.

'I converted it for Mollie,' Albert explained. He opened the double doors, at the far end. 'There she is,' he triumphantly exclaimed.

Albert was clearly one of those men who, having live amidst colliery and industrial grime, suffered withdrawal symptoms on moving to the country. Mollie was his antidote. For she was a beautifully decorated traction engine of the showman's type.

'Made by Charles Burrell of Thetford,' said Albert proudly. 'They made 207 of these – more than anyone else.'

'It's a fine machine,' said Elijah. 'You obviously take great care of it.'

'Oh yes,' said Albert, 'she gets a lot of my time.' Alfred then began to get technical.

'She carries over three hundred gallons of water in its two tanks,' he said, 'so you can go for about twelve miles without a refill.'

'So you could easily get the tin tabernacle from Newbridge to here with just one refill,' ventured Elijah.

'Oh yes,' said Albert. 'And there would be no problem with the tin tabernacle because Mollie can pull up to thirty tons.' Then he said, 'Would you like to go for a spin?'

Elijah had been surprised enough when Derek Hart had treated him to a trip in his beautiful Jowett, but he never dreamt that he would ever ride on such a machine as this.

'If you've got the time, I'd love to,' he said.

'All I need is the excuse,' beamed Albert, and he began to fire up.

When all was ready Albert said, 'Jump up,' Elijah did so, and off they went. As they turned out into the road Albert mused, 'When I lived in the Rhondda Valley – it was about 1925 – I saw a Burrell showman's engine which had run away with its load on Porth Hill. It jack-knifed and that stopped it. Lucky too – there was a big drop off the road.' Elijah could have done without hearing this.

'Oh my!' he spluttered.

'Don't you worry,' said Albert, encouragingly. 'In them days these engines had steel wheels, and that one probably couldn't get a good enough grip on the granite setts. In 1926 the law was changed, and since then these machines have had to be fitted with soft tyres. In any case, we've got no hills around here as steep as that one.'

Somewhat reassured, Elijah began to enjoy the ride. In some places Mollie almost touched the walls on either side of the narrow roads, and when they were negotiating a hairpin bend in a more wooded area they almost reduced the Baptist ministerial ranks by one, for the Reverend Calvin Rowlands, Horeb, came sedately around the corner on his bicycle and took refuge in the ditch. Elijah felt a tinge of pastoral concern, especially since there had been a good deal of rain and it was a crisp December day. Albert had the grace to bring Mollie to a halt. He climbed down and went to Calvin's aid. By now Calvin's teeth were chattering and he was very wet.

'You'll be alright,' said Albert cheerfully. 'You Baptists like a lot of water!'

The Reverend Calvin Rowlands scowled as only a Calvinist can, and when Albert asked, 'Can I give you a lift?' he declined in none-too-polite a fashion. Elijah was on the point of calling out, 'I shall pray for you,' but he thought that would be just rubbing salt in the wound. Instead he said, 'I'm sorry to meet you for the first time in these trying circumstances. Please call and have tea and a chat some time.' But Calvin never did. Albert, Elijah and Mollie resumed their journey and were soon at the Manse, where Albert dropped Elijah off.

Elijah had his Christmas sermons to write; he had to take flowers on behalf of the church to the sick and housebound – of whom there always seemed to be a goodly number at Christmas-time; and he had to ensure that all arrangements were in hand for the highlights of the season: the Nativity Play, the Service of Reading and Carols, and the carol singing around the village. Of these the first two always took place on the Sunday before Christmas.

Elijah had heard that the Nativity Play was always a memorable occasion – and not always because of its primary purpose of conveying the Christmas message. This year was no exception. The elderly Mrs Beatrice Jarman faithfully taught the children their lines, but she humbly confessed that she was quite unskilled in the thespian arts. But Elwyn Roberts was not, and every year he took charge of the production side of the enterprise. He was always slightly reluctant about this because whereas the shepherds and wise men were in the sanction-ridden environment of day school from Mondays to Fridays, on Sundays they were volunteers, and it did not take some of them long to exploit this distinction. He had also noticed that while self-conscious adolescents took a great deal of persuading to improvise on stage, younger shepherds and wise men had no such inhibitions, with the result that on occasion the plot could take quite unexpected turns.

The chapel was bursting at the seams. As well as members of the congregation, some of them with children taking part in the play, there were parents of Sunday School children who did not otherwise associate with the chapel. Some of the latter brought in pushchairs containing the shepherds and wise men of the future, as well as two or three embryonic Marys and Josephs. Some future performers were determined to make their voices heard, and did so. Not for them gold, frankinsense and myrrh:

they were more than content with dummies, rattles and the occasional swig of Cow & Gate. One mother held her baby throughout the proceedings. This was because she was the proud owner of a carriage-built Pedigree pram. ('She's got ideas above her station,' muttered some of the other mothers.) There was simply no room for such a fine conveyance in the chapel, so it had to be parked in the schoolroom in case it were stolen from outside. Not that PC Powell would have had great difficulty in tracing a thief (a) because it was the only such pram for miles around, and (b) because he always patrolled outside the chapel on important occasions when crowds were expected, and even he would have noticed if so grand a pram had been purloined from under his nose.

As usual, Mrs Blodwen Llewellyn, LRAM was at the American organ. Apart from its asthmatic tendencies the organ was a fine piece of work. It was a Corona, made in walnut by The Cornish Company of Washington, New Jersey. It had all the usual stops: diapason, viola, bass coupler, sub bass and the rest; five octaves on the keyboard; and two swell levers operated by the player's knees – a manoeuvre readily and discreetly accomplished by Blodwen underneath her voluminous tweed skirt. Unlike some of its kind, this organ had an impressive upper section in beautifully carved wood. In the centre was a mirror. The organ was situated on the long wall near the front of the chapel, opposite the octapus stove, with which it was sometimes in competition. Blodwen used the mirror as a driver would, for it gave her a good view of what was happening at the pulpit end, and she could even see some way into the congregation, and had more than once seen a slumbering worshipper – especially slumbering farmer worshippers who, on cold winter days, after an hour or two with the animals, would come frozen into the warm, faintly coke-fumey chapel and by the time the sermon started they would feeling so cosy that they were quite unable to keep their eyelids open. On one occasion even Jenkin Jones had succumbed to the enticements of Hypnos the god of sleep, and he was the senior deacon and church secretary. If Dilys had not poked him in the ribs he would not have been able to take the collection. And that would have been a disaster because Dai Cashbox would have jumped into the breach and embarrassed everybody by whispering to each one as he went round, 'See if you can make it a bit more than last week.'

At two twenty-eight Elijah went into the schoolroom to check with Elwyn that all was in order, and that there were no absentee characters. They were all there: Mary, Joseph, shepherds, wise men and angels, but where was the child in charge of props? At that point Mrs Owen rushed in with the sad news that Tim would not be there because his tonsils had flared up again. By what the hymn called 'a frowning providence', Tim was the props boy. What was to be done? At once the Walters twins put up their hands: 'We'll do it,' they said cheerfully in chorus. Elwyn paused. The Walters twins had been banished from the play because of some unauthorised words they had introduced into 'While shepherds watched their flock by night' the previous year. But there was no one else. Elwyn quickly instructed the twins in the one task the props person had to perform during the play, and they looked as dutiful as they could.

With all in order, Elijah went to the pulpit. By now there was a hubbub in the chapel. The parents were in excited conversation, the actors of the future were indulging in what might have been regarded as glossolalia had it been Pentecost. How to create an atmosphere approaching that of worship? Elijah gazed purposefully into Blodwen's mirror and gave her the nod. At that she pulled out all the stops, pushed her knees determinedly on the swell levers, and played a mighty chord. Silence. Elijah called the congregation to worship, said a prayer, and announced the carol, 'Once in royal David's city'.

While everyone was singing, Mary and Joseph came in and stood on the right of the dais below the pulpit. The innkeeper came in and stood on the left. Elijah vacated the pulpit and the angelic host comprising a senior angel and two junior ones took his place.

'Good evening, Innkeeper,' said Joseph. 'We have come a long way and we are tired. Have you got any room in the inn?'

In a way which would have delighted the heart of Stanislavski, the innkeeper immediately left the script and improvised: 'I dunno. I've bin out doin' the milkin'.'

This not being the reply that Joseph expected, he panicked and suddenly needed the lavatory. To cover his absence Blodwen improvised on the script and struck up with 'I'm H-A-P-P-Y' which everybody knew and sang heartily. Meanwhile Elwyn had an urgent word with the innkeeper, and as Joseph came back he whispered to him, 'Ask him again.' So Joseph did, and this time he got a surly, 'No, mate.' At this point Mary embellished her line: 'Are you sure there's nowhere we can stay? I am going to have the baby Jesus soon and Nurse Williams says I must take things easy.'

Nurse Williams visited Mary's home almost as frequently as the post-man, and Mary was well up in antenatal matters.

'Well,' said the inkeeper, grudgingly, 'there's a stable at the back if you don't mind the animals. I'll show you the way.'

With that they all shuffled off, and four shepherds shuffled on with tea towels on their heads and dressing gowns on their bodies. The shepherds sat down to watch their imaginary sheep, and attention turned to the angels in the pulpit. They were standing in an horizontal line, but as she spoke the senior angel took a step forward and raised her arms to show off the wings which her mother has so skilfully made. She said: 'Hello, shep-herds, a baby is going to be born in a stable in Bethlehem. OUCH!! … What did you pinch me for?' she enquired of one of the junior angels.

'Because if you stand there with your arms up our Mams won't be able to see us because of your stupid wings,' came the angelic reply.

While all this was going on of the first shepherd got the giggles. The second shepherd was tickling his feet. Before Elwyn could intervene the senior angel glowered over the pulpit and bellowed at the shepherds, 'Do you want to see this new king, or not?'

'Yes, please,' they chorused, sheepishly.

'Well, then, you'd better get a move on.'

And the shepherds did, the angels following. Out into the schoolroom they went, and then the props boys came into their own. The Walters twins came on to the dais. One carried the manger, the other the baby Jesus wrapped in Mrs Davies's tablecloth. The baby was placed in the manger. Exit the Walters twins. They had performed their duties with such unaccustomed dignity and reverence that Elwyn immediately smelled a rat – with good reason, as it soon turned out.

On came Mary and Joseph. They stood by the manger. On came the shepherds. The first shepherd was due to say, 'We have come to see the new king who has been born.' But the second shepherd was so incensed that he had not been invited to say the line that while they were out in the schoolroom he had given the first shepherd the biggest gobstopper to be found in Hetty's shop. The first shepherd tried to speak. The three other shepherds fell about in mirth and the audience all but lost control of itself. Feeling that the entire performance was at the point of collapse the first shepherd took the only way out. He sidled over to the communion table below the pulpit and spat the gobstopper into the vase containing the flowers. He turned round with a look of triumph on his face and loudly announced, 'We have come to see the new king who has been born.'

'Here he is,' said Mary, and they peered into the manger. They then moved to the side of the dais and knelt in something resembling wonder.

Then on came the three wise men. They each carried a present that they laid at the foot of the manger.

'I bring you gold,' said the first.

After an inordinate amount of rehearsal the second wise man still said, 'I bring you Frank's nonsense.'

'I bring you myrrh,' said the third above his giggles.

'Would you like to see the baby?' asked Mary.

'Yes, please,' said the shepherds and wise men in chorus.

Mary went to the manger, picked up the doll, opened the tablecloth at the doll's head end – and burst into tears as she showed everybody Joey the Clown!

'Wait till I catch those Walters boys,' muttered Elwyn to himself. But they had had the foresight to vacate the building on completing their props work.

The kindly Mrs Jarman rushed to comfort weeping Mary, and Blodwen struck up with 'Away in a manger'. But it wasn't until the final verse that the congregation had sufficiently composed itself to sing with becoming reverence.

Elijah pronounced the benediction and, with a sigh of relief, went to greet everyone at the door. He thought to himself, 'There are times when a minister just has to sit back and let it happen.'

That same evening the Service of Lessons and Carols went off without a hitch. Miss Shirley Morris sang the two solos she had been promised, and everyone was pleased to greet Elwyn's younger brother, Ronald, on leave from armed service in Malaya. He had come to spend Christmas with Elwyn. At the end of the service Elwyn was still inwardly seething about the Walters twins: 'At least Herod was able to slaughter the innocents,' he muttered to himself as he walked out with Ronald into the night.

Two days later the third of the traditional Christmas events took place: carol singing around the village. It was the custom to collect for a worthy cause, and this year the decision was in favour to Dr Barnardo's homes for children. The route was the same each year. It was planned carefully so that after a certain number of cups of tea and glasses of pop the party would find itself on a road with trees on either side: men and boys to the left, women and girls to the right was the drill. The accompanying instrumentalists were the same every year. Mrs Bronwen Llewellyn, LRAM was in charge of them though, as a pianist and organist, she was rather at a disadvantage, neither of her instruments being of the portable type. But some years ago she had purchased an old accordion at a house sale, and this was the one evening per annum when it came out of its box. Having rather elitist musical tastes, she would not normally have given house-room to an accordion, but she managed to persuade herself that lugging that thing around once a year was an aspect of the way of the Cross which she and all Christians were called upon to walk. She had the muscle power for the bellows; she knew nothing at all, and cared even less, about the buttons under the left hand; and although the keyboards on which she made her living were of the horizontal sort, she could manage to play up and down the accordion's keys sufficiently to give no one any excuse for not recognising the tune. She also selected the carols to be sung and, as we shall see, some of her choices for particular houses were more than ordinarily appropriate.

Elwyn Roberts was on the trumpet. He was a skilled player, and in his younger days had been principal trumpeter in the County Youth Orchestra. His colleague, the geography teacher, Charlie Mitton, was the mainstay of the tuba section of the Newbridge Town Band, so he brought some depth to the proceedings. Mary and Hannah Evans of the Sunday School played violins, and Helen James, also of the Sunday School, played the flute. The last instrumentalist was Tommy Thomas. He was the son of Daniel the Headmaster, and his nature, suggested even by the affectionate 'Tommy', could not have been more unlike his father's. In fact

the stuffy Daniel had a number of grouses against his son. He had blond
unruly hair, a scruffy beard and very casual clothes; he was twenty-eight
and still living at home; and he played in one of those new-fangled skiffle
bands in a Newbridge pub. But once a year, without fail, Tommy did his
utmost to tempt a reverent 'Silent night' out of his banjo.

In addition to the players there were the singers: about a dozen
Sunday School children and some members of the congregation. The
band walked off first, the singers followed, with Meirion Hughes bringing up the rear partly because his penetrating, if slightly flat, voice would
drive the singing along, and partly because he was adept at keeping an
eye on any young people who might otherwise have peeled off for other
than carolling purposes.

It was a crisp but bright evening. The moon was out, but they carried
some paraffin lamps in case clouds blew in from the sea. Their first port
of call was always the Rectory. It was a barn of a place – a relic of the
days when rectors had a staff of servants, handymen and gardeners. The
Reverend Aneurin Bentley-Jones had none of these, though he was adept
at making others feel that they were servants of the lowest rank. His wife,
Veronica, could not have been more different. She was a genuine aristo-
crat and therefore had no need to put on airs and graces. 'I can't understand how on earth she let herself get shacked up with him,' Ada Pugh
had once opined to Dilys Jones. Mrs Bentley-Jones was the life and soul
of the Women's Institute, and if there were any pastoral visiting done in
the name of the Parish Church, she did it.

Elijah, as the custom was, went up to the huge front door and pulled
on the bell. Mrs Bentley-Jones opened it.

'Good evening, Mrs Bentley-Jones,' said Elijah. 'I am the Reverend
Elijah Morgan of the Congregational church: I don't think we've met
before; but I expect you know most of our players and singers.'

'I have heard good things about you,' she replied, 'and I hope you will
be very happy here.

'Thank you,' said Elijah. 'We would like to sing a carol to you and your
husband if he is in – and the boys too if they are there.'

'And we'd like a contribution to Dr Barnardos,' said Dai Cashbox, who
was standing by Elijah's side.

'Of course, of course,' she said. 'The boys are with my folk in Ireland' (her husband would have said that they were in the family castle in Ireland, for Veronica was of prominent Anglo-Irish stock). 'But my husband is here. I think he's writing his Christmas Day sermon. I'll call him.'

This she did. The Reverend Aneurin Bentley-Jones put down his copy of *Country Life*, and came to the door.

'Good evening, Sir,' said Elijah. The Rector grunted.

With that Blodwen said, 'I've chosen this one especially for you, Sir.' She counted one-two-three, and brought band and singers in on the famous Welsh tune, 'Olwen'. But Blodwen hadn't chosen the carol for its tune, but for the first line of the words: 'All poor men and humble ...' The Rector gave no appearance of feeling mortified, but at the end his wife smiled sweetly, thanked them, and responded generously when Dai brandished his collecting tin. She said, 'Do come in and have some refreshments.' They did not need to be asked twice.

The pattern was repeated around the village: Elijah would knock, a carol would be sung, Dai would rattle the tin, and refreshments would be enjoyed. As they gathered outside Hannah's shop they rendered, 'Angels from the realms of glory'. There was no ulterior motive in this choice by Blodwen: she liked Hannah and knew that this was her favourite carol. She also liked to witness the contortions into which Charlie Thomas got when trying to accommodate the Gloria to his banjo. A few yards further and they were outside the house of the Baptist organist, Miss Tilly Watkins, ATCL, Blodwen's great rival in the battle for the musical talent of the district. For this carol Blodwen ushered her husband to the front, and Maldwyn dutifully stood beside her. They then launched into 'Unto us is born a Son ...'

A little further on they came to the wall and then to the drive of the Big House. It's proper name was Grantley Manor, the home of Major-General Sir Vivian Brigstock, his wife, Hermione, and their two daughters, Polly and Penny. Like others of his ilk, the Major-General had retired to the country and become a senior churchwarden. He read the lessons in the Parish Church, and was never more animated than when the Philistines were getting a hiding. Then his white handlebar moustache would fairly bristle, his cheeks would redden and his eyes would pop.

No one in church could be in any doubt that he was on the Lord's side. His favourite hymn included the line, 'Christians up and smite them'. For all that, he was a warm-hearted toff and greatly liked in the village, as were all the members of his family. Even Meirion had a grudging affection for him. As an Anglican warden he wasn't too bad, but to Meirion he was Jeckyl and Hyde, for he was also Master of Hounds. It was to him that those requiring baptisms or marriages were directed by the notice board at the Parish Church. The way he dealt with young Lucy Rogers epitomised the coalescence of his pastoral attitude, his military training and his booming voice. Lucy had recently become an unmarried mother, and although her parents had not 'thrown her out', there were those in the village who made their disapproval clear through whisperings and glances. She had approached the large front door in fear and trembling, and said she would like to see the churchwarden. She was ushered into his presence.

'Come in, come in, Old Thing,' he said breezily. 'What can I do for you?'

'Please, Sir,' she ventured, 'I would like my little Melanie to be baptised.'

'Jolly good!' he boomed 'No problem at all. Always good to add new whipper-snappers to the baptismal roll, donechaknow. We'll fix it up in a jiffy.'

'But, Sir,' she stammered, 'I am not married.'

''Pon my soul!' he retorted, 'we can't have the little nipper disadvantaged because of something like that! When unforeseen eventualities arise, change tactics, work a flanker, and press on!'

Lucy was not familiar with the military analogy – or language – but she gathered that there were no insurmountable obstacles. Shortly afterwards little Melanie was baptised at the ancient font, with the Rector going through the motions and the Major-General beaming at Lucy's side.

Hermione Brigstock was a cultured woman, a Roedean girl, who had developed impressive gifts in art – especially painting and tapestry. Her watercolours, sold for good causes, were in many local homes, and she had exhibited in London. Many an Anglican in the diocese blessed her for the comfortable kneelers she had made and decorated. Polly and Penny, though with their mother's good looks – flaxen hair, high cheekbones and good deportment – took more after their father where interests were concerned. There were stables at the Manor, and from these they conducted their School of Equitation. They had passed the examinations of the British Horse Society; they had won numerous prizes at county shows for dressage and show jumping; they gave riding lessons, and in the summer months took parties on pony-trekking holidays. Polly was two years older than Penny and every Christmas, as he stood there with his banjo, Charlie Thomas wondered whether he stood any chance with her but feared, rightly as it happened, that he did not. The sisters spent a good deal of time graciously rebuffing the attentions of upper-class youths who wouldn't know the points of the horse from the points of a compass.

Blodwen had taught Polly and Penny to play the piano when they were younger. They had been among her most gifted pupils, so her choice of carol for this family was perfectly straightforward: 'Hark! the herald angels sing'. Dai Cashbox watched the Major-General as he discreetly put something in the tin, and as it did not drop with a clatter, he knew they had done well there. They all enjoyed the sumptuous spread that Mrs Brigstock had provided, and as he stood there munching her mince pies, Elijah reflected that he had always wanted to learn to ride. 'No chance of that here,' he thought. 'Even if I could afford the lessons, just think how the tongues would wag if I spent any time with either Polly or Penny!'

Their next stop was at the Chart and Compass. It was an ancient hostelry, its name clearly indicating its proximity to the sea. Because of the law, the carollers could not take the children in; and had they violated the law they might not have got Albert the Union out again, carolling night being his most abstemious night of the year. But they always sang a carol by the entrance to the pub, and this year Blodwen had chosen, 'God rest you merry, gentlemen'. It went with a swing, and while they were singing the jovial landlord, Billy Edmunds, came out and some of the regulars with him. There were cheery greeting all round, and Dai's tin reaped the benefit of less than fully clear minds and guilty consciences.

Then came the Baptist Manse, a grey building surrounded by tall trees. It was not in a good state of repair and there was an air of decay all around. Elijah knocked at the door, and Mrs Millicent Rowlands opened it. She was pale, thin, slightly stooped and had a hunted look about her. She looked older than her forty-three years. Elijah asked if they might sing a carol.

'I'm afraid not,' said Millicent, apologetically. 'My husband is having his prayer time in his study, and I dare not disturb him.'

Elijah noted the word, 'dare'. Clearly, the Reverend Calvin Rowlands was one who believed that the man is the head of the house, to be obeyed by all under his command. Certainly Mr Rowlands had never preached on the text which says that husband should love their wives as Christ loved the Church. For all his constant harping on about the fact that we are save by grace and not by law, he conducted all his affairs in a most legalistic spirit, and ruled his family with a rod of iron.

Blodwen was most disappointed that they were not allowed to sing. She had chosen 'Joy to the world' – she had thought that would serve 'the old misery' right!

'I'm so sorry,' said Millicent again. And then she said, 'Wait a minute.' She crept off and a minute later was back with a bag of sweets. As she handed them to Elijah she glanced over her shoulder in case Calvin was emerging from his study. She was safe.

'Please share these among the children,' she said. 'Thank you very much for coming. Happy Christmas to you all.' And with that she closed the door quickly and quietly, so as not to disturb the man of the house, the servant of the Lord.

By long tradition the last port of call was the home of the retired Professor Gareth Reynolds. He lived at the end of a long wooded lane not far past the field in which Tinker Joe and Rowena lived. As they approached the field, Elijah said, 'I would like us to make an extra call this evening – to Tinker Joe and Rowena. I think they would enjoy our playing and singing.'

This had never been done before, and one or two of those present had the country dweller's suspicion of travelling people – even though Tinker Joe and Rowena were well known and had not moved for years.

The oil lamps were lit in the vardo, and smoke was puffing up from the chimney. They gathered on the piece of hard standing, and Elijah said, 'Let's give them "We three kings". The children will enjoy that one.' So off they went, and before they reached the end of the first verse the door opened and Tinker Joe and Rowena came down the steps, while their children in their night clothes stood by the door and watched.

Tinker Joe had his violin with him, and they had never heard such a beautiful descant in the second verse. Rowena and the children joined in the chorus with great glee.

As the carol went along, Elijah sidled up to Dai Cashbox. 'Don't you rattle your tin at him,' he said. 'This is a treat for them to show that we are their friends.' When it was over, Elijah said, 'A happy Christmas to you, Tinker Joe, Rowena and the children.'

'You've made our day,' said Tinker Joe with tears in his eyes. 'We didn't know you was coming, so we wasn't prepared. But are you collecting for something?'

Even Dai Cashbox was too moved to say, 'Yes.' And Elijah said, 'No need for that, we just wanted to come and wish you a happy time.'

'Me and my family wish you all a happy time too, but I still want to see your collecting tin. There are many worse off than us and I know that you try to help them every year.'

'Very well, then,' said Elijah, now feeling that to refuse Tinker Joe's gift would humiliate him; and Dai moved forward with the box into which Tinker Joe put half-a-crown.

Everybody smiled, and then Tinker Joe said, 'Now we'll give you a surprise.' He called Tommy Thomas over and whispered in his ear. Then to violin with banjo accompaniment Rowena danced to 'The Irish Washerwoman.' At the end the carollers cheered and applauded. It had been a really good idea of the minister to call on Tinker Joe and his family.

Eventually they reached Professor Reynolds's house. Everybody knew that he was an unbeliever. Indeed, he had the distinction of being at the top of Meirion's prayer list. But he was not hostile to the churches. He was a distinguished entomologist, and Meirion could never stand outside his house carolling without wrestling with his conscience: 'Should I consort with an advocate of Darwin's theory of evolution?' he would wonder annually. The Professor was a Fellow of the Royal Entomological Society, and his great love was beetles. He could wax lyrical on forest canopy arthropods, and for recreation he would go to the Natural History Museum in London to browse among their millions of mounted specimens. On a number of occasions he had been able to report on a hitherto unrecorded beetle, something which gave him the kind of jubilation normally associated with those who win the pools. And when out on a country walk with friends, whereas they might be admiring the view or the wild flowers, he would dive into any heap of leaf mould that he came across, or gently prod rotting tree stumps. He loved living at Bethel because it had both woodland and seashore species to offer. Within half a mile he could find ground beetles in the woods and maritime ground beetles on the shore – and many more besides.

Blodwen always tried to be sensitive to the Professor's lack of religious convictions when choosing a carol to be sung outside his house. She found it easier to be sympathetic to the humanist than to certain Baptists she could think of. On this occasion she had chosen 'In the bleak mid-winter.' She thought it was not overloaded with doctrine, and she remembered hearing that one theologian had dismissed it as 'Scandinavian moonshine!' It was the best she could do for the humanist.

Elijah knocked on the door, and the Professor appeared. Tall and slightly stooped, he had grey hair, a pointed beard, and thin but cheerful features. He wore a tweed suit, and had a magnifying glass in his hand – he had clearly been inspecting one of his friends.

'How good of you to come to an old pagan like me!' he said, smiling. 'What ditty have you for me this year?'

He soon discovered the answer as Bronwen led them into Rossetti's carol. When they had finished he invited them in. Although he was a widower, he had prepared glasses of pop for the children and something stronger for some of the adults, and ginger cordial for Meirion and his kind. He also handed round a box of biscuits which his sister in Canada sent him every Christmas, and for which he did not much care, though he never told her. Every year the carollers benefited from her generosity.

The refreshments finished he said, 'I enjoyed your music, now I want you to enjoy mine. It's not very Christmassy, but it's fun.'

They followed him out, through the kitchen, to a former stable outside which he had had converted into – what? He flung open the door and said, 'This is where my pride and joy lives!'

The carollers gasped. It was a beautifully restored Gavioli fairground organ with drums and cymbals, numerous pipes, and much else besides.

'Would you like to hear a tune?' asked the Professor.

'Yes, please,' chorused the carollers.

'I haven't any carols, so let's have a good old traditional fairground organ tune.'

He started it up and they stood as if transfixed as it blarted out 'The Carnival of Venice'. It was as if this genial, gracious gent, who spent so much time among creatures of the quieter sort, from time to time needed a compensating blast of sound. Well, with his Gavioli, he certainly had it.

The performance over, he asked Dai Cashbox, 'For whom are you collecting this year?'

'Barnardo's,' said Dai.

'Excellent!' said the Professor. He went into his study, and came out with a £50 note. Dai nearly fainted at the sight. He began to say, 'I'm afraid I can't change …' but the Professor stopped him.

'Nonsense,' he said. 'Put it in your tin. I was a Barnardo's boy.'

They wished him a happy Christmas, and as they walked down the path away from his house the Professor called out, 'If you like, I'd be pleased to take the Youth Club on a beetle hunt when the weather's better.' Elijah made a mental note of that as a programme item not to be overlooked. 'Thank you very much,' he said, and off home, tired and happy, they went.

There was a good turn-out for the Christmas morning service, but after the excitements of the nativity play and the carolling there was a certain sense of anti-climax.

Elijah was well cared for over the Christmas period. As early as 1 December Dilys Jones and Betty Pugh had got into a huddle. The upshot was that with great pastoral sensitivity Dilys invited Elijah for meals on Christmas Day, Betty invited him for meals on Boxing Day. 'We don't want you to be alone in the Manse over Christmas, and we'd love to have you,' they said; and Elijah took them at their word. What he did not know was that there was a protective-cum-pastoral aspect to their plan. They suspected – and they were never wrong in such matters – that if they did not invite the minister early, he would be at the mercy of Mrs Mavis Long and her Angela, or of Mrs Gloria Phillips and her Valerie. Elijah never knew what a narrow shave he had had. But he had a very happy Christmas.

7

The Reverend Elijah Morgan
and the Tin Tabernacle

Early in January the deacons forgathered. After the preliminaries Elijah explained that the main purpose of the meeting was to see how plans for the Grand Concert were coming along.

Elwyn Roberts said, 'The programme is building nicely, and we shall have a few performers from outside our own membership.'

'That's good,' said Dai Cashbox. 'It means that people want to support us in getting a building that will serve the whole village.'

'Quite so,' said Jenkin Jones. 'But we need to make sure we advertise as widely as possible.'

There is a sense in which Jenkin's remark was purely academic, for they all knew that a word in the ear of Hetty at the shop and Billy at the pub would ensure that they could fill the schoolroom three times over.

'I've asked Picasso to get his four best girls making posters – one for Bethel, one for the Parish Church, one for the pub, one for Hetty's shop, and one for the Edwards bus. They will all give date, time, and state the objective of the Concert.'

'What about tickets?' asked Dai Cashbox.

'Arnold Jackson at the *Sentinel* has agreed to print some tickets for us. We'll have some here, Hetty will have some in the shop, and we may be able to find someone with a contact at the Chart and Compass.'

As he uttered the last phrase he looked pointedly at Albert the Union.

'I pass there quite often,' said Albert. 'I'll be happy to drop some in.'

'That's the slowest bit of "passing" I've ever heard of,' muttered Meirion.

'What shall we charge?' asked Dai, ever alive to his financial responsibilities.

'I think for an important event like this we should charge ten bob for adults and five bob for children,' said Jenkin.

'Some people would give a pound if it stopped Madame Myfanwy Price-Edwards from singing,' opined Albert. The others, silently agreeing, looked at him reprovingly, whilst all adopting Jenkin's suggestion.

'How about the refreshments, Mrs Morris?' Jenkin next enquired.

'Everything is in hand,' said Rachel. 'I shall make Welsh cakes, your Dilys will make drop scones, Betty Pugh will make sausage rolls, and Hetty the shop will give us three tins of fancy biscuits left over from Christmas.'

'She'd better not let old Rowland know she's helping us; he'll excommunicate her,' said Albert. Not that Hetty was worried about ministerial retribution. On the contrary, she took a wicked pleasure in circumventing some of her pastor's prejudices.

'As for drinks,' Rachel persisted, 'there will be tea and coffee for the grown-ups and Tizer and Corona for the children.'

'Lovely job,' said Elwyn.

With that Elijah closed the meeting with prayer, and all but one of them went home.

On the last Saturday of January the schoolroom was packed with people, all eager to enjoy the concert and contribute to the tin tabernacle fund. Elijah had been prevailed upon to act as compère, so at seven-thirty sharp he stepped onto the little stage and Mrs Blodwyn Llewellyn, LRAM played a resounding chord which hushed all else. Elijah welcomed everyone and told them that there was a real treat in store; people of all ages would be taking part; and it was all for a good cause. He then announced the first item: three songs by the junior Sunday School children, trained by Mrs Beatrice Jarman.

On to the platform they came, and they sang their hearts out. Over the years Mrs Jarman had gathered an enormous collection of Sunday School songs and services and recitations. She must surely have been one of the most faithful customers of H. E. Nichol of Hull, John T. Hampshire of Dewsbury and John Blackburn of Leeds, whose regularly published songs and words for anniversary services and festivals of all kinds were so eagerly awaited by Sunday School teachers across the land. The children's first song was by Colin Sterne, set to music by H. Ernest Nicholls, MusB (Oxon) himself:

> Happy little children,
> Stand we here today,
> Ready for the Master's service,
> Work or play.

What always happens with such performers, happened. One performer was much more interested in what was going on in the wings. Another was picking his nose, while a third was looking into the audience for her Mummy. But everyone applauded enthusiastically. Building on their success, they treated everyone to two items from Carey Bonner's *Child Songs*: 'For air and sunshine pure and sweet, We thank our Heavenly Father,' and 'A little lamb went straying'. Their contribution over, and Mrs Jarman having insisted upon a dignified departure from the stage, they all marched off the stage like little tin people, their legs and arms as stiff as could be.

From the very youngest members of the church to the very oldest: Fred Nicholls. He was in his nineties; he had fought in the Boer War; he had the white flowing beard and locks of an Old Testament prophet; but he wore the thick tweed suit beloved of those who were, or had been, shepherds. He knew every inch of the hills around Bethel, and he had instructed generations of under-shepherds where to look for missing sheep in snow storms. Now he came forward, his shepherd's crook in his right hand, to deliver his monologue. This he did in a deep, rich voice, ideally suited to squeezing the last ounce of pathos out of the most sentimental words:

> There's a one-eyed yellow idol to the north of Kathmandu;
> There's a little marble cross below the town;
> And a broken-hearted woman tends the grave of 'Mad' Carew,
> While the yellow god forever gazes down.

Maud Williams nudged her husband, Herbert:
    'What a marvellous memory at such a great age,' she whispered.
    But the Williams's were newcomers to Bethel village, and they did not know that old Fred had been reciting that monologue at least once a year ever since it was published in 1911.

After old Fred came Shirley Morris. As it was not a service, Shirley felt it quite in order to be more up-to-date in her choice of solos – which is to say that her songs had been written within the previous fifteen years. First she sang, 'Little man, you've had a busy day' – made famous by Les Allen, but equally adapted to the female voice. Her second choice made some of the more staid church members sit up. She sang 'Bewitched, bothered and bewildered' from the musical play, *Pal Joey*. Mercifully, the version published by Chappell's was edited – for Shirley would never have got away with Lorenz Hart's first verse:

> After one whole quart of brandy
> Like a daisy I awake
> With no Bromo Seltzer handy,
> I don't even shake.

Had she sung that, the light of love in Meirion's eyes would for ever have been extinguished. As it was he stood in the wings, the ever-watchful stage manager, hoping that she was thinking of him as she sang. If she were, she gave no indication of the fact.

So successful had Elwyn's proselytising been, that both Polly and Penny Brigstock from the Big House had volunteered to play the piano, despite the fact that they were 'rusty', and that they would be performing under the eagle eye of their former teacher, Blodwyn. Polly came first and played Schubert's Allegretto in C Minor, and later in the programme Penny successfully negotiated the Allegretto from Haydn's Sonata in G. At the end of each piece the audience applauded enthusiastically, and Blodwyn had the greatest difficulty in remaining seated. Had she not taught them? Ought she not to share the glory? Then she reflected that everyone except the Williamses knew that she had taught the girls, so she contented herself with leaning over to the Joneses and purring, 'See how they both play right into the keys!'

A series of recitations by the older children followed. These were all taken from *Woodland Voices: A Song and Recitation Service* with words by W. Cedric Astle, BA. Young Richard Jarvis had slaved over 'The Squirrel's Store', which began,

From bough to bough, from tree to tree,
The squirrel hops in his elfish glee,
With never a thought of toil or care,
When the summer days are long and fair.

Other children tussled with similar items, and then on came someone who was almost unrecognisable. He was padded out; he wore a bald-head wig, and a suit in Victorian style. If he had not been chasing the Walters twins away from the props cupboard, he would have remembered his shoes. But they quite took his mind off his preparation, so his winkle pickers gave him away. Apart from them, he was every inch Mr Pickwick. And Elwyn performed 'Mr Pickwick on the Ice' with clear enunciation of vowels and articulation of consonants, and admirable timing. It was indeed a masterly performance.

Three musical items ended the first half. First, Jeremiah Parry, custodian of the chapel hymn books which had been donated by his father, mounted the stage to sing that old tear-jerker, 'Just Awearyin' for You'. Known for his acid temperament, and for his skill at chasing the Walters twins away from his apple trees, the audience could hardly believe that it was Jeremiah. His singing was not as skilful, but he gave his all, and he was applauded with mingled astonishment and relief. Then Mrs Blodwen Llewellyn, LRAM came into he own. She played 'In a Persian Market,' by Albert W. Ketèlby, whose name sounded so foreign – but not as foreign as his psudonym, Anton Vodorinski – but who, in any case, was born in Birmingham. Blodwen played with such imagination that the audience could almost see the camels approaching, the beautiful princess, the jugglers, the snake charmers and the beggars. Finally, to the surprise and delight of all, Elijah announced that the final act of the first half was to be Tinker Joe and Rowena. Tinker Joe played 'Widow Machree,' to which Rowena danced an Irish jig. They finished to thunderous applause, and then came the refreshments. PC Powell, who was there in his public safety capacity, but who had nevertheless made a generous donation to the tin tabernacle fund, rose to his full height and said,

'There's so many folk in here that there will be accidents if you all move towards the food at once. Stay in your seats and food and drink will be passed along to you. When you have been served, you can stand up and stretch your legs.' Unable to disagree with PC Powell's assessment of the situation, and by nature unwilling to go against the voice of the law, the women of the catering committee summoned the deacons, and together they served the people where they sat. It was all very efficient and safe.

The second half opened in boisterous fashion. With a certain amount of trepidation, Elijah introduced the first act as The Bethel Chapel Stompers. They had never been heard of before, and they would probably never be heard of again. But for this special money-raising occasion, there they were. Elwyn was on the trumpet; Charlie Mitton from the town band was on the tuba; Tommy Thomas had his banjo; and Elwyn had press-ganged two senior pupils from the school, Frank Smith on clarinet and Susan Jeremiah on trombone. Blodwyn had been persuaded to swallow her principles and play the piano and – who was that on the washboard? Why! The Minister! At the sight of Elijah with his 'instrument' there was much wagging of tongues in the audience. Meirion, standing in the wings, wondered how he could pretend to be somewhere else: the devil's music on chapel premises!! They delivered themselves of an adaptation of Harry Gold's arrangement of 'At the Jazz Band Ball', and they really swung it. Elwyn excelled with Freddy Tomasso's trumpet solo, while Susan Jeremiah handled Geoff Love's trombone solo with aplomb. The audience was not exactly hopping – one would not expect that of a Bethel chapel audience; but most of them had beams on their faces, and a few were gently and rhythmically jigging up and down in their seats. At one point even Meirion felt his left foot tapping in time to the music. He stopped it at once, and felt quite ashamed of himself.

When the applause finally died down, Elijah relieved himself of his washboard, removed his thimbles, and announced that the next on the list was Mr Derek Hart from the garage. 'But he's not here tonight to talk about cars, but to mystify you. As some of you know he is a member of the Magic Circle. So please welcome master-magician, Derek Hart.'

Derek came on to the stage with his props. They could hardly recognise him. Some of them had never seen him without his overalls, but here he was in smart evening dress with a stiff white shirt and bow tie. There was not a smudge of grease to be seen on his face. He was truly a skilful conjurer, and not the least of the attraction to him of the magic arts was the fact that they tested his designing and manufacturing skills. For he would make many of his more elaborate props himself. He had children on the stage whom he amazed with his close-up card tricks; he brought the rabbit out of the hat; his volunteers never guessed under which tumbler the golf ball would be; he tore up white paper, rolled it in his hand, said the magic words and a white dove appeared. But on this occasion the pièce de resistance was his magic cabinet. Of his own invention, it was a fine piece of craftsmanship. He wheeled it on – all seven feet of it – with Meirion helping him. As Meirion made to leave the stage, Derek said, 'Don't go, I'm going to make you disappear!'

'Thank God for that!' said Albert the Union, involutarily, in the audience, whereupon he sustained a very sharp nudge in the ribs from Ada's elbow.

Meirion looked more than faintly alarmed, but he could not protest – after all, it was for a good cause. With a great flourish Derek ushered him into the cabinet and closed the door. He turned the cabinet on its wheels to show that there were no escape doors, waved his wand, said the magic words, and opened the door. No Meirion was to be seen. Thunderous applause as Derek took his bow and wheeled the cabinet off stage.

'Where did Meirion go?' Dilys asked Jenkin.

'How do I know – it's magic,' came the not-very-informative reply.

At that point, Meirion returned to the schoolroom through the front door, to still further applause, and resumed his stage-managing position in the wings.

Next up were the members of the Youth Club. Coached by Elwyn, they gave a spirited rendering in chorus of Robert Browning's poem, 'How they brought the Good News from Ghent to Aix'. Then came Susan Jeremiah's clarinet solo to Blodwyn's accompaniment. She played the Grave and Adagio from Giuseppe Tartini's *Concertino*, which had just come on the market in an arrangement by Gordon Jacob. It was beautifully done. She was followed by Daniel Thomas the Headmaster, who gave a soulful rendering of 'If those lips could only speak' – a song which suited his breathy tone and his doleful face to perfection.

The youngest soloist of the evening was Jenkin and Dilys's grandson, Noah Jones. It was his first public performance, and Blodwen his teacher had done her best to eradicate nerves and encourage concentration on the job in hand. He strode purposefully to the piano, sat down, plonked his music on the stand, and off he went. He introduced his own items. In a loud, clear voice he said, 'I'm going to play "The Jolly Farmer" by Walter Carroll.' On hearing the title the first thing Albert the Union thought of was the pub in the next village. By the time he thought again, young Noah was more than halfway through. 'My second piece,' he said, 'is "The Woodpecker" by Lavena Wood.' Noah knew about woodpeckers, and he was able to make this percussive piece come alive – and did so, to enthusiastic applause.

Then it was Elwyn's turn. He could play many instruments, and now he came on to the stage with his English concertina. The audience expected something from the folk clubs, and were surprised, and entranced, when he nodded to Blodwen at the piano, and they treated the audience to a most sensitive performance of Regondi's Serenade in A, with its Introduction in A minor, and its lively Allegretto Scherzoso.

Elijah thanked them warmly, and then he said, 'Now there's something we haven't had yet. We've had reciters, singers, players, a conjurer; but we haven't had a comedian. Well, we've got one know. Please give a warm welcome to Albert the Union!' And they did.

Albert had a long-standing interest in the music-hall tradition, as well as in comedy on the wireless. He had a sizeable collection of records by various variety artists, and he had memorised many of these. When despatched from the Valleys to London for Union meetings, he would always make for the Palladium for the evening show. He had seen Tommy Trinder, the Crazy Gang, and many more. He could not only remember their lines, he was an accomplished mimic, as we shall see.

Having briefed Blodwyn and Elijah, he opened in true music-hall style. He came on to the stage looking very serious and said, 'Good evening ladies and gentlemen. Tonight, for your delectation, I shall render "Only a rose".' With that he nodded to Blodwen, who played a chord. And then, with Elijah rushing on, it went like this:

'Only a rose I …'

'I say, I say, I say! My dog's got no nose.'

'How does he smell?'

'Terrible!'

'I don't wish to know that. Kindly leave the stage.'

After two or three similar interruptions, Albert moved on to higher (or at least less corny) things, and introduced his audience to the Sage of Hogsnorton, Mr Gillie Potter. He donned a boater, picked up a rolled umbrella, put on a deadpan expression, and spoke in precise, clipped English, as he impersonated the celebrated son of a Wesleyan minister and native of Chipping Sodbury, whose accounts of the doings in his imaginary village were appreciated far and wide by the discerning. Albert had perfect recall of a script he had heard many times on his Columbia (5067) record. It was a lengthy monologue concerning a visit to Southend.

'Good evening England. This is Gillie Potter speaking to you in English.' After many scrapes, Potter ended in the most fashionable restaurant in Southend. 'I'm sorry I can't tell you the name of the restaurant: I've left the spoon at home. But I remember I had the best half-crown dinner for a guinea that I've ever had anywhere … I said, "How much is the bread?" The waitress said, "The bread is free, we throw that in." I said, "How much is the gravy?" She said, "The gravy is free, we throw that in." I said, "You throw an awful lot of stuff in in the course of a day, don't you?" So I had bread and gravy. Then the waiter came with the bill – five pounds twelve. For a moment I thought he'd overlooked something. I said, "This is rather an alarming bill for the small quantity I've had. What is the twelve shillings for?" He said, "That's for the fruit." I said, "I had no fruit." He said, "No, but it was there if you wanted it." I said, "Would you fetch the manager, please?" So they went out to find the manager in the restaurant to which he goes to have his meals. And when he was conscious I spoke to him. I said, "What is the meaning of this bill? For what exactly does the twelve shillings stand?" He said, "That's for the fruit." I said, "But I had no fruit." He said, "No, but it was there if you wanted it." So I took the bill and took off five pounds, gave him twelve shillings. He said, "Why have you done that? Why have you taken off five pounds?" I said, "That was for kissing my wife." He said, "But I didn't kiss you wife." I said, "No, but she was there if you wanted it."'

The applause in some quarters was qualified by what the more prim and proper thought was a risqué punchline. But worse was to come.

Albert's favourite comedian of all was the 'Cheeky Chappie', Max Miller. It had been a highlight of his Union career when, on 29 December 1943, he had seen Max at the Palladium. He could not remember whether Max told tonight's joke on that occasion, but he knew it could have been told by nobody else. He caught Miller's swiftly spoken, aggressive, 'smart Alec' style exactly:

'My wife come 'ome late last night. She'd bin to the pictures. Bin to the pictures. I said, "Did you 'ave a good time?" She said, "I 'ad to move me seat three times!" I said, "Did you get accosted?" She said ...'

By now, Meirion was in a sweat in the wings. Having the smut-detecting antennae that are characteristic of the patheologically pious, he divined that something horrible was coming. So before Albert could say, 'Eventually!' Meirion rushed to the electric meter, pulled the switch and plunged the schoolroom into darkness.

'OOOOh!' said the audience in surprise. Meirion switched on his torch and ushered Albert from the stage. Constable Powell rose from his seat and said in the most commanding tones, 'Let's not have any panic. Stay where you are until further instructions are forthcoming.' So they did.

With Albert back in his seat, and Meirion back in the wings, Meirion returned to the meter, and switched the lights back on. Elijah resumed his role of compère, and said, 'Now we have a great contrast – there could hardly have been a greater. It is my privilege to introduce Madame Myfanwy Price-Edwards.' The artiste came on to the stage, and as she did so, Dai Cashbox quietly left the room and made for the chapel vestry. Everybody knew why. He was off to count the takings so that he could announce the result before the end of the concert. He did the same at the Harvest Service and Sale, and he always chose the most suitable period to absent himself: from the sermon at harvest time, and from the diva tonight.

Madame Myfanwy was undeniably a presence – and she warbled her way through two of the 'old favourites': 'If I were a blackbird' ['You're an old crow', muttered Albert to himself; and, indeed, Madame Myfanwy was swathed in black flowing – even multi-layered – garments from head to toe]; and Franz Lehar's 'Vilia'. For her encore – for she would never leave until she had given an encore, hence the loud applause she received – she launched into 'In the Gloaming', whereupon the light bulb failed above her head. Perhaps it was the shock of the earlier black-out, but the bulb's timing was excellent. In the half-light from the kitchen Madame Myfanwy, old trooper that she was, gave her all and completed her task with a display of vibrato the like of which had never been heard before, even at Bethel chapel.

As she left the stage, Meirion appeared with a new bulb, and light was restored. Then Elijah announced the final item of the evening. 'The men deacons will now perform two spirituals: "Go down Moses" and "Steal Away". And so they did. Jenkin Jones and Dai Cashbox did their best to hold the melody line; Meirion was a wavering tenor; Elwyn sang second tenor; and Albert supported them all with his deep bass voice. When it was over, Elijah said, 'I think that Dai Cashbox has something to tell us.'

Dai stepped forward from the male chorus, and resumed his more regular role.

'Yes,' he said. 'It's good news. With tickets, refreshments and donations we've made £42.' They all cheered, while Dai thought, 'With the twenty from chapel funds that makes £62. We're well over half way, but where will the £38 come from – and then there's the transport of the tin tabernacle.'

But even as he was thinking this, Blodwyn played the chord, and they all stood for the National Anthem.

On the first Wednesday in February the deacons forgathered. The preliminaries over, Jenkin said, 'Now we must take stock about the tin tabernacle.'

'We've done very well so far, but there's a good way to go,' said Dai, his brow furrowed with worry.

'Well, now,' said Jenkin, 'at our last meeting the minister told you that I'd heard a little whisper. I'd now like our minister to say something about that.'

They all looked at Elijah, and he said, 'We have received a letter from Messrs Williams, Davies and Jones, Solicitors, of Newbridge, and this is what it says:

We are pleased to inform you that the late Mrs Ellen Roderick has willed the sum of £500 to Bethel Congregational Church. This sum of money will be passed to your appointed financial officer if he or she will kindly call at the above address.

There was a stunned silence, followed by an air of jubilation. Jenkin brought them down to earth.

'This is a real godsend,' he said. 'Now we can make our plans. I will write to the Roman Catholics and tell them that we shall arrange to transport the tin tabernacle on the last Saturday of March. Is that convenient to you, Albert?' he asked, remembering that Albert and Mollie would be involved from Newbridge Station.

'That's fine,' said Albert.

'In the meantime,' Jenkin continued, 'we must get the base for the tabernacle made.'

Dai said, 'I've got contacts in the building trade who could help us out with materials for the base.'

'And I can get my big roller on the job,' Jenkin added. 'Let's make a start next Saturday.'

Elijah said, 'We can't for ever keep calling our new building a tin tabernacle. I propose that we call it Roderick Hall, in memory of Mrs Roderick.' To this suggestion there was unanimous agreement.

'What we need is a proper opening ceremony,' said Elwyn.

'I've been thinking about that too,' said Elijah. 'We ought to have a fairly short dedication service, followed by a free entertainment.'

'Why "free"?' asked Dai, as sharp as a pin.

'As an expression of thanks to all those who helped with the fund,' said Elijah. When it was put like that, Dai could say no more without sounding too mean for words.

'I think it would be fitting,' said Elijah, 'if we were have the dedication service outside Roderick Hall, and then open the doors and all go in together.'

'Excellent,' said Jenkin, and they all agreed.

'And,' Elijah continued, 'it would be right to invite Roderick, Salem, to say a few words.'

Roderick, Salem's longest 'few words' being a price well worth paying for £500, there was unanimity on the point.

'Now, what about the entertainment?' asked Elijah. 'It needs to be pleasant but not rowdy.'

'Somewhere between the sublime and the gorblimey,' said Albert, culprit of the Grand Concert.

'Quite so,' said Elijah.

'I could ask Charlie Mitton to see if the Newbridge Town Band would give us a concert after the opening service,' Elwyn volunteered.

'Just the job,' said Jenkin, and it was agreed.

So all the arrangements were made. On the next few Saturdays the men prepared the base for Roderick Hall. Jenkin's treasured Fordson Model F tractor with the roller attached levelled the brick and rubble from Dai's contacts in the building trade, and a final layer of cement was laid on the top.

On the last Saturday in March Roderick Hall was transported by rail to Newbridge, and Albert and Mollie brought it the last seven miles, with Elijah serving as Albert's assistant. All available men were on hand to unload the sections, and on the Monday Jenkin, Dai, Albert and other available men erected the building. It was in good structural order, though it would need a coat of paint when the weather became more settled. But it was useable henceforth.

When the work was almost complete, Roderick, Salem, drove up in his old Morris.

'What a wonderful sight!' he exclaimed as he saw the tabernacle. 'My mother would have been so proud of it.' They showed him around – not that there was much to see, because there as yet were no furnishings: it was an empty shell with a stage. But that was soon remedied, for in total they had £562 available. The tabernacle cost £100 and its transport, £25 (Albert, of course, charged nothing). That left more than enough for chairs, a table, some curtains for the stage, and various other items that all such places need.

'Come with me,' said Roderick, Salem, to Elijah, and they walked to the car. Roderick opened the rear door and pulled out a large sign bearing the words, 'RODERICK HALL'.

'There,' he said, 'I've had it painted in town, and it's my personal gift in memory of my mother.' Elijah thanked him warmly, invited him to say 'a few words' at the opening on the second Saturday in April, and the men fixed the sign on the porch above the front door.

Happily, the second Saturday in April was a bright, if somewhat chilly, day. The church members and numerous other well-wishers from the village gathered outside Roderick Hall. Constable Powell performed his usual feat of moving people off the narrow road, Mrs Rachel Morris was busy with the ladies in the room at the back of the hall, preparing the refreshments, and the Newbridge Town Band musicians were unpacking their instruments and warming them up in the schoolroom. Their director, Gwyndaf John, had agreed that the band would accompany the opening hymn. When all was ready, Elijah and Roderick, Salem, stood by the porch. The band formed up next, followed by the deacons and all the people.

Elijah then said to the assembled company, 'It gives me great pleasure to welcome you all here today. Many of you have contributed to the purchase of this hall, but we could not have completed the task without the generous gift left to us by the late Mrs Roderick. She served this chapel faithfully all her long life, and this building will be a fitting memorial to her, and also a means whereby Bethel can advance its work and serve its community. I now invite the Reverend John Roderick, the late Mrs Roderick's eldest son, to declare the hall, named after his mother, officially open.'

Roderick, Salem, was not going to content himself with just declaring the building open. Far from it. He likened the erection of the tabernacle to the building of Solomon's temple.

'Solomon didn't have my Mollie,' mused Albert the Union, while Elijah, more biblically, hoped that Roderick Hall would be spared the destructive attention of Nebucadrezzar and the Babylonians.

'Its dimensions were perfect for its purpose,' Roderick, Salem, continued, as if he himself had once ministered there. And he described in detail, and with no a little embroidery, the view from the courtyard and the furnishings within. Eventually he came to that eternal temple, not made with hands, which awaited all Christians in heaven. And he wondered how many of those present that afternoon he would see there (tacitly assuming that he would be there). This led him on to encouragements to the faithful and warnings to the ungodly (at which point the second trombone looked a little sheepish); and he finally remembered what he had come to do:

'I solemnly declare Roderick Hall open. May it be a blessing to all who use it, and a fit instrument for the Lord's work.'

By now many of those gathered were shivering, but they took heart when Elijah nodded to Gwyndaf John. He raised his baton, and the band crashed into 'Now thank we all our God'. Roderick, Salem, opened the porch door and the band marched in. They looked very smart in the royal blue uniforms with gold braid on the collars and cuffs. They were in the third section of brass bands, but they always did their best. Marching and playing at the same time – in fact, just marching – was not among their accomplishments, so some set off on the left foot, others on the right. Jones the Chopper, Newbridge's finest butcher, who always had a bright red face, looked positively incandescent as he walked, hugged his huge B flat bass, and blew. They walked the length of the hall and mounted the stage, where their music stands were already in place. Roderick, Salem, and Elijah and the deacons and the rest of the people followed them, and took their padded seats – a novelty at Bethel chapel, but the late Mrs Roderick had provided.

As people behind were settling in, Elijah looked at the band. By now he knew a number of them, and there seemed to be an interesting correlation between the size and shape of the performers and the instruments on which they performed. Thus Jones the Chopper was a huge man, entirely suited to his instrument, as was his neighbour, whose name Elijah did not know, but he had seen him humping tree trunks in the wood yard in town. Some of the cornet players seemed lean and hungry-looking, and Elijah knew that two of them were accountants; others of them had a radiance about them which suggested that they had first played under the auspices of the Salvation Army. The tenor horn section was entirely female, and Elijah knew that he had seen one of them in uniform on the hospital wards; the others might have been nurses or teachers. The baritone and euphonium players included a plumber, a gardener and a farmer. The trombonists were the most deceptive of all. The most that could be said of them was that having the most widely-useable instrument, and judging from their reddish-blue gills, it was a reasonable assumption that two of the three of them also played jazz in Newbridge's hostelries, and were rewarded in liquid kind.

They opened with Sousa's 'The Washington Post'. Thereafter they played a number of pieces, with refreshments intervening at the appropriate point. The programme included 'Holiday Suite' by Eric Ball, a selection from Edward German's *Merrie England*, and Eric Ball's march, 'Sure and Steadfast'. They finished with Edwin Wigglesworth's hymn tune to the words, 'Praise ye the Lord' – as played by the Besses o' th' Barn Band. The name of this famous band was well known to many of the Newbridge players, though some would have been hard put to say where Besses was. The audience was most appreciative, and Harry Mortimer himself would have been proud of the band. Elijah expressed the thanks of all, and the first memorable event of many in Roderick Hall was over.

It would be quite wrong to suppose that Elijah's thoughts were exclusively directed to the tin tabernacle during the first months of the year. On the contrary, he had sermons and Bible study talks to write. He was invited by Daniel Thomas to speak at the school assembly, and there were always pastoral visits to be made, some of them to hospital. It was a busy life, and getting from place to place was very time-consuming. He became a familiar sight on Edwards Brothers' bus but, of course, they just went to town and back. Elijah had to visit people up long farm tracks and down even longer side roads. Then one day Derek Hart telephoned him.

'I told you I'd be thinking about you,' he said, 'and now I've got just the thing. Come down to the garage when you're free and have a look at it.'

Elijah had promised to make two visits that afternoon, but as soon as they were done he went to the garage.

'There she is,' said Derek. 'That would get you round your flock very nicely. It's secondhand, but I've known it from new, and I've looked after it. The first owner recently got married and his wife won't go near it, so he's had to buy a car. It's in perfect order. What do you think?'

Elijah was almost too stunned to think anything. He was gazing at a shiny Matchless 350 motor cycle. He knew his stipend would not cover such a purchase.

'Do you like it?' asked Derek.

'It's grand,' said Elijah, 'but I could never afford it.'

'There's no need to think about that now,' said Derek. 'One step at a time.' And he went on to explain that he would not sell the bike to Elijah until he was sure that he liked it and could ride it properly. Then he would ask Elijah to pay him £2 per month over three years – interest free. Elijah said, 'That's really very generous of you.'

'Well,' said Derek, 'I know I'm not very regular at the chapel these days. But I was in the Sunday School, and my late Mam would like me to help the minister in any way I can.'

With that, Derek began to explain the working of the machine, and Elijah began to look increasingly bemused as he heard about oil pump filters and plungers, cams and tappets and the like. Derek noticed the glazed look and said, 'Well, that's enough of that. Plenty of time to explain things if you decide to go ahead. How about it?'

Elijah said, 'It really would be so useful – yes! I'll do it.'

Derek then explained that there were a few things to be done before he could take the machine away. He would need third party insurance; a three month provisional licence; and he would need some suitable clothes.

'Where can I get clothes from in this area?' he asked.

'The best place is Harry Harris's in Newbridge,' said Derek. 'But make sure you go for good quality gear. Here, borrow this Barbour catalogue.'

'Thanks,' said Elijah. 'I'll study this and get the paper work done.' And off he went. That evening after tea he almost missed the starting time of the Bible study because he was so engrossed in Barbour's catalogue. It was a new world to him. There were superweave thornproof jackets with a map pocket and two skirt pockets; trousers reinforced at the inside leg seams for the purposes of kick-starting the engine; there were short gauntlets, goggles and helmets. Fortunately Elijah had a birthday in the offing, and his relatives were always eager to buy him something he really wanted. So, to their considerable surprise, he distributed the above items amongst them, and in due course they arrived in the post one by one.

The paperwork attended to, Elijah became a learner motorcyclist. With Derek's help he made a start. He soon learned such slogans as 'Don't flood the engine', and his confidence gradually increased. After his more successful practice rides he would say to himself, with reference to the Old Testament character of whom it was said that 'he drives furiously', 'If I keep this up I shall soon be known as the Jehu of Bethel.' It would be some time, however, before he would be ready to take his test.

8

The Reverend Elijah Morgan
Receives a Visitor and Pays a Visit

In the midst of all the preparations for the January Grand Concert, Elijah
had received two phone calls. The first was from Principal Morgan Mac-
Donald of the Theological College. After pleasantries regarding Elijah's
progress at Bethel, the Principal said, 'Now I wonder if you can help me?
We have an American research student here at the moment, and he needs
somewhere to stay over the Easter vacation. Do you think one of your
members would put him up? He was ordained two years ago, so he could
be useful to you in various ways. His name is Oscar J. Brownsberger III,
and he's from Oklahoma.'

'I'll be glad to see what I can do,' said Elijah, thinking that among all
the Joneses, Williamses, Daviesses and the rest a Brownsberger would at
least have some novelty value.

Elijah was wise enough to raise the matter with the deacons when next
they forgathered: it would have looked like favouritism if he had simply
asked one family to give the American hospitality. So he explained the
situation to the deacons, and at once Jenkin said, 'Dilys and me'll be glad
to have him: it'll do him good to see a farm that covers acres, not miles.'
So it was agreed – and Jenkin and Dilys would have been first on Elijah's
list anyway.

Oscar duly arrived at Newbridge Station, where Elijah met him.
Except during the holiday season, crowds were never large at the station;
but it would have been easy to pick Oscar out however large the crowd.
He was very tall, thin but with a wiry strength; he was wearing a ten
gallon hat, and carrying a large suitcase. His hair was the colour of ripe
corn, and he had a moustache to match. As soon as he spoke it was clear

110

that he was not from Wales. Elijah welcomed him warmly, and then gave him his first experience of the Edwards Brothers' bus. On arriving at Bethel, they walked up the hill to Top Farm, where Oscar received yet another cordial welcome from Jenkin and Dilys.

Oscar threw himself into the life of Bethel. He gave some Sunday School lessons; he went around the hospital wards with Elijah; he helped Jenkin out on the farm and thoroughly enjoyed a trip to Newbridge Market; and on one of his three Sundays he conducted the services. As he stood in the pulpit, and in accordance with their custom, Mrs Mavis Long thought, 'He'd be great for my Angela,' while Mrs Gloria Phillips could just see Oscar and her Valerie sharing a Manse together somewhere. But then the cat was set among the pigeons, for Oscar and Angela fell in love at first sight! It was the talk of the village for weeks afterwards, as Angela prepared for a wedding at Bethel at the end of Oscar's research year, and for subsequent departure to his pastorate in Guthrie, Oklahoma.

Mrs Gloria Phillips had mixed feelings. On the one hand, her Valerie had lost out; on the other hand, the competition for Elijah was reduced by fifty per cent. And she had heard that Elijah was going to have a motorbike. She could just see her Valerie on the pillion …

The deacons forgathered. Jenkin said, 'This Oscar's a fine chap. He's been very helpful to us all. We must give him a good send-off. We'll have a social evening.'

All the usual preparations were made, with Mrs Rachel Roberts being in charge of the refreshments.

Elijah said, 'Let us make Oscar the star of the evening.'

'We know he can preach,' said Dai Cashbox, 'but what can he do at a social?'

'Well,' said Elijah, 'he has a wonderful collection of slides of Oklahoma. I'm sure he would be pleased to show them to us – and we could see where Angela Long will be living.'

'I'll borrow the school's projector,' said Elwyn.

They all thought this a splendid idea, and Oscar was more than happy to oblige. A large company gathered for the social, and Oscar presented his programme. He first of all gave them a potted history of his state. He told them how on 16 September 1893 the Cherokee Outlet had been opened up and more than 100,000 people raced from all quarters to occupy some of the six million available acres of land. Some 40,000 of them were successful. They settled on the land and built homes and churches. The Congregationalists had their Northwestern Academy at Carrier in Garfield County as early as 1898; and they also had a College at Kingfisher.

Oscar then described the terrain.

'Have you heard of John Steinbeck?' he asked. Nobody had. 'Have any of you seen the film, *The Grapes of Wrath*?'

'Oh yes,' a number replied in chorus, and Mavis Long sighed, 'Wasn't Henry Fonda lovely?'

'Well,' said Oscar, 'that film was made from John Steinbeck's novel about the depression years and drought conditions which gave Oklahoma its reputation as the dust bowl. But that's not fair, because four neighbouring states also suffered drought in those terrible years. Since then a programme of water damning projects and the creation of lakes has given Oklahoma more water than any other landlocked state. Yet people still think of it as the dust bowl.' With that, he showed the first slide.

'This here is where I was born,' he said in his casual Southern drawl, as he showed a picture of Helena. 'It's Alfalfa County, and it's mostly fields. It was established just a year after the opening up of the Cherokee Outlet.'

'What's the population?' asked Dai Cashbox.

'Between six and eight hundred,' Oscar replied. 'You can see farmland stretching out flat for miles, and the summer temperature can easily reach 110 degrees. We're in what's known as Tornado Alley, and these tornados can be quite scary: you can see them coming towards you in the distance, and if one comes really close, the only thing to do is to make for the basement and hope for the best.'

Oscar then showed a picture of a larger town.

'This is Alva,' he said. 'It grew up quickly during the rush for land. The folk arrived in the area in September 1893, and by November one hundred and thirteen businesses had been set up. Some people from Kansas dismantled their homes, carted them to Alva, and re-erected them. By 1907 Alva had a fine Opera House.'

Oscar showed a number of other slides of Alva, and then he said, 'Now this is the Northwestern Oklahoma State University. It's where I got my BA in English and History. It was started with just two teachers and sixty-six students in 1897. Its building was known as the Castle on the Hill, but that was destroyed by fire in 1935.'

'Not too far from Alva is the Great Salt Plains Lake.' He showed pictures of the Lake, and of the 11,000 acres of surrounding salt flats. 'This,' he continued, 'is the only place in the world where you can dig for selenite crystals which include hourglass sand.'

'What's it like for wildlife, with all that salt?' asked Elwyn.

'At any time of year you can see white-tailed deer and quail. In the winter, cranes and bald eagles visit, and we also get heron, geese, ducks, kingfishers, woodpeckers pelicans, and lots more besides.'

Oscar then explained that after his first degree he went to Phillips Theological Seminary in Enid, where he gained his BD.

'How do you think the city of Enid got its name?' he asked.

'Well, it's a girl's name,' said Mrs Morris, 'but I don't know who she was.'

'I can't tell you either.' said Oscar. 'One tale tells how one of the first officials in the new city was a great fan of Tennyson's "Idylls of the Kings", and he felt that Geraint's wife deserved to have a town named after her. But another story is that when in 1893 it was still a place of tents, a cowboy went to the cook tent and turned the sign DINE back to front.'

He proceeded to show slides of Enid, and especially of the campus of Phillips University. He had some particularly fine images of Henry Lee Willet's beautiful stained glass windows in the Mary E. Bivins Memorial Chapel.

'While I was at the seminary,' said Oscar, 'there was a big celebration in the Enid Convention Hall to mark the publication of the Revised Standard Version of the Bible. More than three thousand folks came to the event, and Phillips University was represented by the former President, Dr I. N. McCash and the chaplain, Walter Moore.'

'Now,' Oscar continued, 'You'll be wanting to see where Angela and I will be living.' So he showed pictures of Guthrie. 'Guthrie was the state capital until 1910,' he said, 'and it has some fine buildings.' He showed them the offices of the Cooperative Publishing Company, the largest Masonic Temple in the world, the City Hall, the Carnegie Library, the Federal Building, and the site of the biggest employer, the Oklahoma Furniture Manufacturing Company. Finally he showed them pictures of his Manse, a nicely appointed timber framed dwelling, and of the church. By Bethel's standards, it was imposing indeed, with its tower, its expensive interior furnishings, and its halls and rooms of varying dimensions.

Altogether it was a most informative evening, and Angela in particular had paid the closest possible attention. The slides all shown, Oscar thanked everyone for the warm welcome they had given him, and he then produced some duplicated sheets on which he had typed some traditional recipes.

'Here are some ideas for your next lot of refreshments,' he said as they pored over the ingredients of the Oklahoma Casserole, the Dinner-in-a-pumpkin, Oklahoma Cherry Dessert, and Sourdough Bread.

The next day Oscar returned for his final term at the university. But for some time after his departure the children of Bethel village could be heard greeting one another with a heartfelt, 'Howdy!'

The second phone call Elijah had received during January was from his College friend, Jeremy Ellis. 'How would you like to conduct our Sunday School Anniversary services here at Zion on the first Sunday in May?' Jeremy asked.

Thoughts rushed into Elijah's mind: Jeremy had taken a church in the Black Country; he himself had never been more than a mile or two out of Wales; this was a great opportunity; he would have to go by train because he would not have passed his motor cycle test by then ...

'I'd love to do it,' he said eagerly.

'Excellent!' said Jeremy. 'You can stay with Jenny and me. But you must come on the Friday in order to attend one of my religious festivals. I'll tell you all about that later. You won't have to do anything.'

So it was agreed. On the appointed Friday Elijah took the Edwards Brothers' bus but to Newbridge, and then took trains via Bristol to Birmingham. There was Jeremy to meet him, his face as cheerful as ever below his mop of curly black hair. Outside the station was his Triumph

Herald (a wedding present from Jenny's solicitor father). They clambered in, and Jeremy set off for his Manse by a circuitous route. As they went along Jeremy told Elijah about the fascinating territory he and Jenny now inhabited.

'It's called the Black Country because of the smoke and grime of the industrial revolution,' he said. 'But it would be better called the Black Countries. It's quite wrong to think of it as an area of homogenous, dull industries. There's great variety. It's really a complex of towns of various sizes, and lots of villages and hamlets, all of them fiercely independent, and with hills and valleys separating some of them from others.'

'What is the main industry?' asked Elijah

'Well, the area was founded on the South Staffordshire coalfield,' said Jeremy, 'and iron and lime were very important too. So we have coal mining and smelting works. But what's really interesting is the amazing number of smaller industries, some of them identified with particular communities. Everyone's heard of Willenhall locks, but there's also Brierley Hill glass, Dudley nails, and Walsall leather.'

'There seem to be a lot of chapels too,' Elijah remarked.

'There are dozens of them,' Jeremy responded. 'There are former Wesleyan, New Connexion and Primitive Methodist chapels. They were supposed to have united in 1932, and they did – on paper. But around here many of them still think that they are what they were before union. Then there are Baptist Union chapels, Strict and Particular Baptist Chapels, and Gospel Standard Baptist Chapels, as well as a few Congregational chapels and an historic Unitarian one at Coseley.'

'I suppose they are all fiercely independent too?' said Elijah.

'Yes. Some of them are still fighting the eighteenth-century battles between the Calvinists and the Arminians. In fact, we even have battles between Calvinists and Calvinists. In one place there is a Gospel Standard chapel at the top of a long hill, a Strict Baptist chapel half way down, and the Methodist chapel at the bottom. The Calvinists at the top take the degrees of height above sea level as indicating proximity to heaven – so the Strict Baptists have some way to go, while the Arminians are well and truly at the bottom!'

'It seems to work in all fields, this independent spirit,' Elijah remarked.

'I've already seen a branch of the Dudley Building Society, the Rowley Regis Building Society and the Tipton and Coseley Building Society.'

'Exactly!' Jeremy agreed. 'And there's great and usually friendly rivalry between the numerous male voice choirs, amateur dramatic societies and amateur operatic societies. They all perform quite regularly. And I would guess that in Holy Week Stainer's *Crucifixion* and Maunder's *Olivet to Calvary* are heard by a greater proportion of the population here than anywhere else in the country.'

'It seems to be the kind of place that would throw up some real characters,' mused Elijah.

'You can say that again!' said Jeremy, and he went on to relate the story of the Tipton Slasher. 'His real name was William Perry. He left canal work for prize fighting and became the British champion. There's even a poem about his life and death. It's quite long. I can only remember the last verse, not because of it's poetic quality, but because I heard it recited by a dentally challenged chap whose sibilants were exaggerated. It goes like this:

> And if you have a tear to shed,
> Friend let it be a splasher!
> And let it fall for him now dead,
> The gallant Tipton Slasher.'

'Not the greatest verse, I agree,' said Elijah.

'Of course,' Jeremy observed, 'we don't only remember fighters around here. There were some pretty eccentric ministers too. Pastor William Bridge, the strict Calvinist of Coppice Baptist chapel, Coseley, was one of them. He always preached in a black silk gown – unusual among Baptist pastors of the time. In 1816 he was "Appointed as minister during his natural life," and he continued there until he died in 1861. There's a book by John Freeman called *Black Country Folk* in which Freeman tells a number of stories about Bridge. One day his wife infuriated him by selling a chest of drawers and buying an expensive bonnet with the proceeds. The following Sunday she arrived late in church. Bridge stopped in mid flight and said, "Here comes my wife with a chest of drawers on her head."

'On one occasion he made the difficult journey to London. He first caught the canal boat, *The Swift Packet* to Birmingham, and from there went on by stage coaches. He preached for some weeks in London, and as the Baptists there bade him farewell, they gave him a currant loaf. He did not eat it on the journey, but took it home. He carefully cut it in his kitchen and out rolled a number of gold coins, given by the Londoners in appreciation of his ministry, and hidden in the loaf to fool brigands along homeward route.'

Warming to his theme, Jeremy continued, 'Freeman also recalls Henry Higginson of Bilston. He was known as the Roving Ranter. He preached all over the area, but quite regularly had meals with one family where the menu was invariably rabbit. For grace before the meal one day he said,

> Rabbits young, and rabbits old,
> Rabbits hot and rabbits cold,
> Rabbits tender and rabbits tough,
> I thank Thee, Lord, I've had enough.

After this the menu changed, so his next grace was:

> For this roast beef and apple tart,
> I thank Thee, Lord, with all my heart.'

By now they had reached Jeremy's Manse. Jenny came to the door to greet them. Elijah had seen her before at College functions, but he did not know her well. She was petite, with long auburn hair. She and Jeremy had met through the University tennis club. Following a degree in Modern Languages she had trained as a librarian. Now she was working full-time in the local library, much to the consternation of some of the women of the church, who thought it unnatural that the minister's wife should do anything other than preside at their meetings, visit the sick, and make cakes for the sale of work.

'Let's have something to eat,' said Jeremy. 'We mustn't be too long, we've got this religious festival to attend.'

After an enjoyable meal they were off in the Triumph again, and to Elijah's surprise they arrived at Monmore Stadium in Wolverhampton.

'What are we doing here?' he asked.

'I come here every week,' said Jeremy. 'Wouldn't miss it for the world. It's speedway! I support the Wolverhampton Wasps.'

Elijah had never before been to such an event.

As they parked the car and walked to their seats in the stand, Jeremy said, 'Each team has seven riders, and fifteen races make up the match. The The Wasps' colours are black and gold. The bikes have no brakes ...'

'No brakes?' Elijah expostulated in horror, thinking of the state he would be in if his Matchless had no brakes. 'It must be really dangerous.'

'Well, the riders need to have plenty of skill,' Jeremy agreed, 'and sometimes accidents happen. Last season there were three fatalities across the country.'

'How long is a race?' asked Elijah.

'Four laps,' Jeremy replied, 'and here each lap is 329 yards. Vic Emms and Ron Mountford hold the record: four laps in sixty-seven seconds.'

By now they were seated. Then the teams came out in turn and circled the track in an introductory way. Jeremy pointed out the brothers Jim and Les Tolley, and lamented the fact that before the end of the previous season Harry Bastable had been sold to the Birmingham team for £1,000. 'That's the main reason we came seventh out of nine teams in division two at the end of last season,' he mourned.

The introductory laps completed, the race was on. Elijah found it quite exciting, though it seemed to him that the rider who was first into the first bend usually won. It was certainly fast and furious, and the smell of petrol fumes and hot cinders was something he had never experienced before. For all their efforts, the Wasps lost the match.

There was not much about a team almost at the bottom of the second division to appeal to the crowds, so support evaporated at the stadium. Few had Jeremy's dedication, and Elijah felt for him when it was announced that there would be no more speedway in Wolverhampton. It was to be ten years before it returned.

The following day was one of the busiest Saturdays of Elijah's life. Gordon Hancox, one of Jeremy's deacons had connections with the operation of the system of canals (locally, 'cuts') in the Midlands, and he had arranged a trip for Jeremy, Elijah and a few of his own friends through the famous Dudley tunnel on the section from Parkhead to Tipton. The commercial use of the tunnel had ceased in 1950, and it had been closed on grounds of safety. But occasionally special groups of cavers and others were allowed in. With Gordon as their guide the party was in good hands. He knew every inch of the tunnel. As they set off he outlined the early history of the tunnel:

'The tunnel was built by Lord Dudley to connect his limestone mines on Castle Hill to the Birmingham canal at Tipton Green. They planned the route from above, and sunk about twelve construction shafts along it. Then they dug in from below and horses pulled the earth and rubble up the shafts to be disposed of above. Because of the nature of the limestone, a good deal of the tunnel had to be bricked up as they went along. It took about three years to make, and it was finished in 1778. The main tunnel is a mile and three-quarters long.'

Gordon pointed out points of interest along the route. 'We're now in the Gaol,' he said as they passed through the narrowest part of the tunnel. 'Now here comes the Bulge' – and they could see the bulge in the tunnel roof, and carefully skirted it. From Basalt Cavern they could see light at either end of the tunnel, and when they reached Limestone Cavern Gordon said, 'We've now left the coal measures behind.' They passed by Hurst's Cavern, a former limestone mine, through the spectacular Cathedral Arch in which boats of up to thirty-five feet in length could turn around, through Tipton Tunnel and out at Tipton Portal. The party disembarked and disbursed, with profuse thanks to Gordon.

Jeremy and Elijah then walked back to Castle Hill. From the top they had a glorious view of the Black Country in one direction, and of the Worcestershire and Shropshire countryside in another.

'The story goes,' said Jeremy, 'that Dudo the Saxon built a castle here around AD 700. Nothing is known of it now. Later, William the Conqueror created William FitzAnsculph the first Baron of Dudley, and he built a castle here about 1080. It was demolished during the Civil War in 1647, and finally destroyed by fire in 1750.'

Elijah was glad that his companion had a first degree in history. He came from somewhere near Carmarthen, but had clearly soaked up the local history and culture.

'But now see what has happened!' said Jeremy. 'Since 1937 the area around the old castle has been a zoo!'

And so it was, and the two of them spent more than an hour looking at the range of animals, birds, reptiles and fish which were on display. Then Jeremy said, 'Now lets go and get a hot pork sandwich from Bellfield's in Castle Street.' So that is what they did. 'It was invented by Bellfields by accident, really,' said Jeremy. 'A customer who was late for work couldn't stop to eat in, so in haste some pork was cut, stuffing and gravy were added, and the first famous Hot Pork Sandwich saw the light of day. It immediately became a very popular snack.'

'It's certainly very tasty,' said Elijah.

When they had finished, Jeremy said, 'Well, this morning we were underground and then on top of the hill; now we'll go and do something more peaceful. Let's go and watch some bowls.'

'Good idea,' said Elijah, wondering how many more examples of local culture Jeremy would be able to fit into the day.

They set off for Villiers Avenue, Bilston, the home ground of Bilston Town Bowling Club. By the time they arrived the match had already started. As they walked into the ground the first thing Elijah noticed was that players were bowling across the green at a great variety of angles. He also guessed that the centre of the green was about nine inches higher than the edges. He had never seen such a green before. Indeed, he had hardly ever seen a bowling match before, but when he had, the bowlers kept to links and played up and down in more or less straight lines; and the greens were as flat as billiard table tops.

While Elijah was thus pondering the scene before him, a cheerful-looking, stocky, man bustled towards them.

'Hello, Joe,' said Jeremy. 'I thought we'd find you here.' And he proceeded to introduce Elijah to Joe Darby, one of his staunch church members who was also a great fan of Bilston Town Bowling Club. They found a bench to sit on.

'Now Joe,' said Jeremy, 'explain to our visitor what's going on.' And Joe obliged.

'This game is called Crown Green Bowling, and we're in the Willenhall and District League of the Staffordshire Association. It's an old Association. It was a founder member of the British Crown Green Bowling Association in 1907.'

'Remind us of the rules,' said Jeremy.

'Well,' Joe replied, 'a match consists of fifteen ends, and in each end two players bowl against one another, and each plays two woods. The woods are biased and so is the jack. When bowling, players must keep their toe on the little rubber mat – we call it the footer, and the winner of an end is the one who has one or two woods closest to the jack.'

They watched for a while, and Elijah gradually got the idea of the game.

'Now watch him closely,' said Joe at one point. 'He's Mr Minns. He was recently the runner up in the F. W. Collins Cup; and in 1950 our G. Turner won it.'

The game went on, and then Joe said, 'Today we're playing Rubery Owen. They're a very good team. They've won the Challenge Cup for the last two years – but we won the Consolation Cup last year.'

Elijah thought that there could not be a greater contrast between this peaceful scene and the noise and danger of the speedway. It wasn't likely that anyone would get killed playing bowls, though from time to time he detected a certain rising sense of frustration in some of the players whose woods had not rolled as intended – often because they has 'lost their legs' and stopped short.

There were hearty cheers all round when the home team beat their rivals. Joe Darby was beside himself with glee; tears of rejoicing came into his eyes; and even if they could not manage quite the same emotional commitment, Jeremy and Elijah clapped heartily and said how much they had enjoyed the match.

Back they went to the Manse for tea, and Elijah supposed that he would have the evening quietly to compose himself for the Sunday School Anniversary – the real reason for his presence in the area. No such thing! After tea Jeremy and Jenny took him to a Black Country Night Out at one of the local church halls.

The hall was full. The members of the audience were seated at tables (Elijah wondered why), and on the stage were four rows of seats with some space in front. No sooner were they seated than the Master of Ceremonies came on to begin the proceedings.

'Ladies and Gentlemen – good evening,' he said. 'Good evening', they all replied. 'Tonight we've got a real treat for you,' he continued. 'The

Black Country's favourite choir: The Coseley Male Voice Choir. Let's give them a real Black Country welcome.'

The choristers – some thirty of them aged from eighteen to eighty – marched onto the stage and took their places. The applause was deafening: they were clearly very popular, and in the seven years of their existence they had made a great name for themselves.

'They really are excellent,' said Jeremy. 'Not just their performances, but their attitude. They give a lot of their proceeds to charity, and they will support the smallest society or chapel, or sing to hundreds in Dudley Town Hall.'

Elijah noticed that on the platform was their banner with its motto, 'Fellowship in Song'. The accompanist played an introduction, and the choir launched into that most dramatic piece by De Rille, 'The Martyrs of the Arena'. It told the story of Christians being thrown to the lions in Rome. They did not recant, but were upheld by their prayers, sure in the knowledge that 'death is the dawning of endless light'. Among other well-known items they sang Hugh Roberton's 'All in the April Evening', Martin Shaw's 'With a Voice of Singing', and Sullivan's 'The long day closes'. There were tenor and bass solos, and the negro spirituals, 'Steal Away' and 'Sometimes I feel like a Motherless Child'. A particular favourite with the audience was the Welsh hymn tune, 'Gwahoddiad', which made Elijah, Jenny and Jeremy feel quite at home.

At intervals between the items some Black Country comedians took the stage. It was clear that some of their material had been heard before, but somehow the audience's anticipation of what was coming made it all the more fun. Elijah soon discovered that many of the region's jokes concerned Aynuk and Ayli:

> Aynuk said to Ayli, 'You look a bit down in the mouth, mate.'
> 'Ar, I've lost me dog an' I cor find 'im nowhere.
> 'Why doh yo put an ad in the paper?'
> 'Doh be daft, our dog cor read.'

There was much more in this vein, and the audience responded with great glee.

About halfway through it became clear what the tables were for. Elijah was sitting near the gangway on one side, and during the interval a woman came up to him and said, 'Are yo 'avin' soom faggits 'n' mooshy paese?'

Elijah's ears were not sufficiently accustomed to the local accent, so Jeremy spoke for them all: 'We'll all have it,' he said, 'and three teas too, please.'

In a flash the woman returned with three steaming plates of faggots and mushy peas, and three mugfulls of tea.

Elijah did not know what to expect from a faggot, and he had no idea what its constituents were. But it tasted really good.

'How do you like your meal?' asked Jenny.

'It's great!' said Elijah with such enthusiasm that a man at the next table leaned across and said, 'It's more than great, it's historic. The Hills of Walsall have making these to the same recipe since 1888.'

At the end of the evening the choir left the stage, and the audience slowly left the hall. As they reached the door they were offered the choice of a bag of homemade toffee or a bag of pork scratchings to help them on their homeward way. But Elijah and his friends were too full for any further culinary experimentation, so they returned to the Manse and tumbled into bed.

The following morning Elijah awoke early, and collected his thoughts for the three forthcoming services. From the Manse window he could see the chapel across the road. It was a sizeable building, and it was surrounded by a graveyard. He could hardly believe his eyes. All over the graveyard there were people gathering up grave chippings, putting them in buckets, and making off with them.

'What's the meaning of that?' he asked at breakfast.

'Oh,' said Jeremy, 'everything has to be spick and span for the Sunday School Anniversary – even the graves. They take the stone chippings home and wash them, and put them back before the service.'

After they had eaten, Jeremy explained the order of the day's events. He would conduct the services, and Elijah would preach in the morning, talk to the children in the afternoon service, and preach again in the evening.

At the morning and afternoon services the children occupied tiered rows that had been built in front of the high pulpit. The girls all had new white dresses for the occasion, the boys had new white shirts and coloured ties. During the first two services they contributed numerous items – so many, in fact, that Elijah wondered whether there would be time for him to preach. There were songs by the youngest children; songs by the older children; song by the boys; songs by the girls; and a number of recitations as well. The evening service followed the more normal order, many of the children by now being too exhausted to do any more performing.

The chapel was packed for every service – the gallery as well as the ground floor, and it took a long time to gather in the offerings of the people. Just before the evening sermon, Zion's equivalent of Dai Cashbox crept out to count the day's money. He returned as the sermon ended, and before the final hymn Jeremy invited him to the pulpit to announce the result. 'This year, we've done better than ever,' he said. 'The sum of £178 has been given today.'

At that the organist broke into, 'Praise God from whom all blessings flow', Jeremy offer a closing prayer, and the final hymn and blessing concluded what all agreed was a most successful day.

Back in the Manse, Elijah, thinking how envious Dai Cashbox would have been, said, 'That was a remarkable amount of money in one day.'

'Oh yes,' said Jeremy. 'We don't get that every week! In fact many of the people there today came from miles around. They or their children used to be in the Sunday School, perhaps, and they want to support its work. Because all the proceeds of this day will finance the children's work for the next twelve months – and then we'll have another Anniversary.'

'I thought the children did very well,' said Elijah. 'Some of them had a lot to learn.'

'Yes, they did,' Jeremy replied. And next week they'll do it all again because it seems a shame to put all that effort in for one Sunday only. But, of course, next week we won't have a visiting preacher, they'll have to make do with me.'

'That will be no hardship, I'm sure,' said Elijah, remembering the high praise Jeremy had received from Professor Geraint Jenkins following one of his sermons in Sermon Class: 'Bung ho! Just the ticket, old chap,' the Professor had chirrupped.

The following morning, after fond farewells, Elijah returned to Bethel. His mind roamed around the many new experiences he had had in those few days. At one point one of the Aynuk and Ayli jokes came into his mind, and he laughed out loud, much to the surprise of his fellow passengers.

9

The Reverend Elijah Morgan's
Summer Activities

During the first week of June the deacons forgathered. The preliminary business over, Elijah's first task was to report on his visit to London. He had represented Bethel at the May Meetings – the annual Assembly of the Congregational Union of England and Wales. He thought it quite remarkable that whereas up to the end of April he had never been out of Wales in his life, in May he had been first to the Black Country and then to London.

'It was a very impressive occasion,' he said. 'We met in Westminster Chapel – the largest Congregational chapel I've ever seen. It has two galleries and a huge bandstand of a pulpit. And it was packed with folk from all across the land.'

He gave an account of the inspiring, elegant, address given by the incoming Chairman; he said how moving it was to hear the roll call of ministers who had died since last they had met in Assembly; and how humbled and proud he felt when he, along with all the other newly ordained ministers, was welcomed on the platform by the Chairman.

'The Moderator from every Province introduced those who had newly come to his territory,' he explained. 'So I and young John Roderick were introduced by our Moderator, and Jeremy Ellis up in the Black Country was introduced by the West Midlands one.'

Elijah reported on some of the debates he had heard, and was particularly inspired by the evening meeting devoted to the London Missionary Society. Missionaries from as far afield as the South Seas, Madagascar and British Guiana had spoken about their work, and it was all very exciting.

'What about the Union's finances?' asked Dai Cashbox – as might have been expected.

'Oh, I think the Union will survive for another year or more,' said Elijah, emulating Dai's own minimalist financial reporting. Elijah was sure he would have heard of any monetary disasters in conversation around the chapel, but in fact he had played truant during the financial business and had visited Westminster Abbey. And on another evening he had gone with young Roderick and Jeremy to see Agatha Christie's play, *The Mousetrap*, at The Ambassador's Theatre. He saw no reason to arouse the ire of the ultra-Nonconformist Albert the Union by referring to his visit to the Abbey, or to kindle the pious disdain of Meirion by mentioning what would no doubt be branded a thespian den of iniquity.

His report over, Elijah came to the main business of the evening.

'I think it would be a grand idea,' he said, 'if we took the members of our Youth Club on a camping holiday.'

'I think it would be a good idea if *you* took them,' said Albert with some emphasis.

'Oh yes,' Elijah retorted, 'I am more than willing to go on this adventure.'

'They'll have to pay their own way,' said Dai Cashbox.

'Of course,' said Elijah.

'Where will they go?' asked Jenkin.

'We'll go to my part of Wales,' said Elijah. 'I know a farmer in the Glasbury area who would be willing to give us a field to camp in.'

'I'll come with you,' said Elwyn, willing to give up a week of his school holiday rather than have his minister subjected to the waywardness of youth all on his own.

'Living in a field won't do his winkle pickers any good,' thought Meirion, a malign smile spreading across his face.

'You'll need a woman leader too,' said Mrs Rachel Morris, 'to look after the girls.'

Elijah could only with great difficulty envisage the staid and quite elderly Mrs Morris roughing it under canvas.

'Oh, I don't mean me,' she bristled, as if reading his thoughts. 'I'll find someone.'

'What about equipment' asked Jenkin.

'The Scoutmaster in Newbridge would lent us tents, billycans and other necessities,' said Elijah, 'and we could hire the Edwards Brothers' coach to take us and bring us back. That, together with a contribution towards food, would be the only charge on the campers themselves.'

So all was agreed.

Later that week Elijah heard a knock at the Manse door, and there stood Valerie Phillips. Valerie was a pretty twenty-two-year-old, with long dark hair and sparkling eyes. She was heading for promotion in the bank in Newbridge.

'I have a small pastoral problem,' she said.

'Do come in', said Elijah, wondering what it could be. Valerie clearly looked rather embarrassed.

'Well, it's like this,' she said. 'Mrs Morris has told my Mother that there is nobody better suited to look after the girls at camp than me.'

Elijah began to tremble inwardly. He had overheard Mrs Gloria Phillips say how nice Valerie would look on his pillion. Valerie, somewhat flustered, blurted out the next sentence at double speed,

'Now I know my Mam thinks of me as bait to catch you, and I just want to say that you're quite safe.'

'So are you!' said Elijah with such equal rapidity that it did not seem entirely gallant.

'That's all right, then,' said Valerie.

The air thus cleared, they discussed plans for the camp. It turned out that Valerie had camped before with the Girl Guides, and also that she was a cook of the adaptable sort needed for such excursions. She volunteered to buy the food, and Elijah booked the coach and arranged for the tents and other equipment to be picked up in Newbridge on the way.

The day came, the Youth Club members were there in force. The Club was for children between the ages of twelve and sixteen – 'A providential age range,' thought Elijah, 'seeing that the Walters twins are eleven.' There were sufficient young people of each sex to fill the promised bell tents – and off they went. The Scoutmaster in Newbridge was on hand to help load the equipment, and after that they did not stop until they reached George Jarvis's farm. Elijah, Elwyn and Valerie called at the old half-timbered farmhouse, and Mrs Emma Jarvis rustled up lemonade and biscuits for all the travellers. Then they began to set up camp.

Bob Edwards helped them unload the food and equipment from the coach, and then he set off for home.

'Rather you than me,' he said to Elijah with a huge grin; and as the coach left the farm Elijah thought, 'Nothing for it now: we'll have to stay and get on with it.'

George Jarvis helped Elijah and Elwyn pitch the tents, while Valerie and Emma superintended the stuffing of the palliasses with fresh straw. There was a wood at the bottom of the field, and there the lads dug the latrines, while the girls unpacked the cooking utensils and food. Then they all gathered wood for their camp fire.

Hetty at the shop had given them twenty-four cans of soup, and Valerie heated up sufficient of these while the girls buttered bread and the boys kicked a ball around.

'Keep it well away from the tents and fire,' said Elwyn in his Deputy Headmaster voice; and they did.

That night the young people did not get to sleep very early, which meant that the adults didn't either.

'Watch out for the mouse I put into one of your palliasses,' said Matthew Bellis as the girls went into their tent for the night – an injunction which prompted much giggling and sifting through straw, and all to no effect.

During their holiday they played games; they sang songs around the camp fire in the evenings, and every night Elijah would end the proceedings with a Bible reading and a prayer. But he also told them something of the history of the Welsh Marches, and he read them extracts from the diary of the Reverend Francis Kilvert, who had ministered in the very area where they were camping. It will surprise nobody who has ever camped with young people to learn that the best received extract concerned an assistant curate who had come to Talgarth. A bilingual man had been requested, but the newcomer's Welsh was not very good. So when at a marriage service he should have asked whether anyone knew of any lawful impediment 'why these two persons may not lawfully be joined together in Holy Matrimony,' what he actually said was, 'why these two backsides may not be joined together in Holy Matrimony.'

There were many fine walks in the area, and Elijah knew them well. One day they walked on a section of Offa's Dyke. They could see the

Black Mountains clearly, and Elijah told them the legend of the Old Lady of the Black Mountains, who would entice walkers to their deaths in the mist or at night, unless they placed a bowl of water by Craswall maypole. They investigated the Hillock of the Graves, a Bronze Age tumulus, and passed the site of the battle of 1093 between Rhys ap Teudwr and the English. Hundreds died, and it is said that the Dulas Brook was blood-coloured for three days.

As they walked, Elijah told them some more tales about Francis Kilvert – how on one occasion in 1870 he had gone to preach at Bettws on a Sunday afternoon. It was very cold. He wore two waistcoats, two coats, a muffler and a mackintosh, and still felt cold. His moustache and whiskers were stiff with ice, and his beard was frozen to his coat. There was a baptism, and the water in the font had turned to ice, so they had to break it, and the baby was baptised with ice swimming about in the font. At Clyro he told them of the generosity of a Miss Beynon, who had financed the building of a Congregational chapel there, and a house for the care-taker. She had also left a sum of money to reimburse the minister from Hay, who was required to preach in Clyro regularly on Sunday afternoons.

For Elijah, the highlight of the holiday was the visit to Maesyronen Chapel on the Sunday. In 1697 local Dissenters had modified a barn near the village of Ffynon Gynnedd, and turned it into a meeting house. As he stood outside, looking at the chapel with the sun shining down upon it, Elijah could hear the excitable voice of Professor Geraint Pritchard:

'Ah! the saints of old! What courage was theirs. How firm their faith! Whose heart does not leap on hearing the names of Vavasor Powell, Walter Cradoc, William Erbury, and the martyr John Penry? Think also of lesser known ones: David and Mary Preece and nine others hauled before the magistrates in Brecon in 1687 for not attending the Parish Church for three Sundays running! What an unforgivable imposition upon the Lord's people! Think too of those whose names are quite unrecorded in our his-tory, but listed in the Lamb's Book of Life! Recall also with thanksgiving the Toleration Act of 1689. It gave our forebears freedom to worship in accordance with their consciences, but no older Acts were repealed. They were still second class citizens, debarred from civic service, from the universities, from the professions. But the Lord was with them, and

Maesyronen was one of their early sanctuaries of prayer and praise. Think of the noble work accomplished by Henry Maurice as he visited scattered companies of saints, travelling from Llanigon over the Black Mountains to Crickhowell in all weathers, and leading worship in the original Maesyronen barn!'

On such mixtures of fact and sanctified opinion Elijah had been reared. These were his people, and Maesyronen was his place too. They went into the chapel, and Elijah pointed out its interesting features: the pulpit on the long wall in true meeting house style; the three box pews; and the large oak table around which the members sat for the Lord's Supper, passing the bread on its pewter plate and the wine in its two-handled pewter chalice from one to the other.

Farmer and Mrs Jarvis had friends at Ffynon Gynnydd, and they had alerted them to the visitation of Elijah and his Youth Club. This meant that two things customary in Wales happened. First, during the service the minister asked Elijah to come up and 'say a few words'. This he did, to the complete satisfaction of all. Secondly, the moment the service ended, as if from nowhere, tea and refreshments were produced, and the members of the congregation and their visitors all tucked in together. In all, it was a very happy time. What was not expected was the consternation caused when it was learned that the organist would not be there on account of a sick relative. But, providentially, Valerie was there, and she had been a pupil of Mrs Blodwen Llewellyn, LRAM, and no harmonium, however unfamiliar and even wayward, could hold terrors for anyone of whom that could be said. So the hymns went with a swing.

By the next Saturday they were back at Bethel, having thanked the Jarvises, and having had a wonderful time. Some of the young people had acquired more blisters in that week that in all the rest of their lives to date. But they could hardly complain after all they had heard about the saints of old who had tramped so many miles for the sake of the gospel.

On opening the Manse door, Elijah found a pile of post, and also a note from Jenkin and Dilys Jones, Top Farm. It read, 'Please come to lunch and tea tomorrow. Our daughter Glenys is here from Canada with her husband Ron.' So after the morning service Elijah made his way up the hill to the farm.

It turned out that Glenys had met Ron during the war. She had been a Flight Officer in the Women's Auxiliary Air Force, and Squadron Leader Ronald MacDonald had been stationed in England with the Royal Canadian Air Force. Now they lived in Okotoks, Alberta – a place of which Elijah had never heard before.

'It's about twenty-five miles south of Calgary,' said Ron. 'We can always go there if we need something special, but it's amazing how many facilities we have in Okotoks.'

'What do you do?' asked Elijah.

'I'm afraid that after the war I became that boring thing, a tax accountant,' Ron replied.

'I keep him well away from my books,' Jenkin interjected.

'How do you like it there, Glenys?'

'It's great!' she said with real enthusiasm. It's quite rural, as Bethel is, but it's countryside on the grand scale.' With that she rummaged in her bag and brought out some photographs. 'This is the Big Rock, just outside of Okotoks. And this is the spectacular Elbow Falls.'

'One of our favourite places', said Ron, 'is Bragg Creek. It's just like a small frontier town. Then there's the Kananaskis Country with its hills, lakes and rivers, and in the winter its snow-covered mountains.'

'What animals live in the area?' asked Elijah.

'We have bear, elk, beaver and moose,' Ron replied and as he did so, Glenys went upstairs and returned with a tin of moose meat for Elijah. He received it gratefully, thinking, 'This will be a first!'

Then Glenys showed him more photos of the area, and he said

'It seems to be a place of ancient natural phenomena and modern human developments.'

'Exactly,' said Ron. 'The first inhabitants of Calgary arrived only eighty years ago – an army encampment. And there's still a pioneering flavour to the place. People have always come from somewhere else, and the friendliness of these towns and villages is is, I think, because when they first came, everyone needed a bit of help from those already there.'

'Now look at this,' said Glenys, and she showed Elijah pictures of the famous Calgary Stampede.

'Have you been to it?' he asked.

'Oh, yes,' said Glenys. 'There's always a lot to see there quite apart from the cowboys and rodeo shows. And we all try to catch the spirit by dressing in Western clothes – even in church during Stampede week.'

With that Dilys called them to the tea table, and then they all went to the evening service.

On the following Saturday there was a Bethel event of prime importance: the annual Sunday School Outing. By long tradition children and parents, and anyone else who wished to join the party went by the Edwards Brothers' coach to Newtown-on-Sea. Mrs Beatrice Jarman, the Sunday School Superintendent, always presided; there were always mothers who told their little children not to be sick on the bus – something their off-spring had not thought of being until the possibility was suggested to them – and then they were! The minister always had a free ride, and Dai Cashbox hired the coach every year, and every year complained that the cost had risen yet again.

Newtown-on-Sea was a fairly presentable place. It had been a prom-inent fishing port in days gone by, but since the war it had been re-inventing itself as an ideal place for holidays. There was a holiday camp there, and for day trippers there were plenty of things to do, and plenty of places to shelter if it rained, which it frequently did.

The younger children made a dash for the beach, brandishing their buckets and spades. They made sand castles, splashed about in the water, ate toffee apples and ice cream, and became increasingly grubby as the day wore on. The older ones made for the fairground, where there were bumper cars, a switchback, a ghost train, and gallopers with a beautiful mechanical organ in the middle. The adults who had no children to worry about listened to the band on the bandstand, or played clock golf.

Halfway through the afternoon the heavens opened, and everyone made for the pier. The youngsters watched a traditional Punch and Judy show. They all seemed to enjoy it, except that when the dentally profuse crocodile came up behind Punch, little Lottie Evans howled the place down, and needed the lavatory at once. The older children found their way to the penny arcade. The Win a Chew machine, which rewarded the successful with Wrigley's chewing gum, was a great favourite – except with the Edwards brothers who, at the end of the day, had to remove a good deal of it from under the coach seats. There were games where pennies were rolled onto numbered squares and mechanical grab cranes selected prizes, and there were Shoot the Rabbit stalls where moving targets could be hit with prize-winning consequences. The older members of the party made for the Lilac Room, where they were entertained by Jacques Vallez and his Savoyards. Mr Vallez was famed for his much appreciated solos on the saw.

At six o'clock sharp, they all made their way to the coach. Well, that was the idea, but where were the Walters twins? That was the other thing that happened every year. Those rascals were always mischievously employed, and therefore always late. On this occasion they arrived with a policeman in tow.

'Do these belong to you?' the constable asked Mrs Jarman.

'In a manner of speaking, they do,' she replied politely.

'I was called to a shop where they had been up to mischief,' said the constable.

'What did they do?'

'One of them went to the back of the shop and called out, "OOOh! look at the size of this rat in the corner!" As the shopkeeper left the counter to investigate the other one filled his pockets with sweets and cigarettes. Do these rascals have names?'

'Of course they have names,' Mrs Jarman replied, 'Why do you ask?'

'Because they told me that they did not know who they were.'

'What made them say that?'

'They said they had been abandoned by their parents before they were a year old, and had been brought up by wolves in the forest.'

'Oh dear,' said Mrs Jarman, trying to look reproving, and trying equally hard not to admire the twins' nerve. 'Leave them with us,' she said, 'and we'll take them well away from your beat.'

'You've made my day!' he said, and off he went, satisfied that henceforth Newtown-on-Sea would be that much more law-abiding because of his vigilance.

Elijah pondered the tall story the twins had peddled to the constable and, good Latinist that he was, he recalled the story of the feral twins

Romulus and Remus. 'That's as close to a classical education as those Walters twins will ever get,' he thought.

The journey home was uneventful except that the air was filled with noisy renderings of songs – none of them from the Bethel Chapel chorus book. Indeed, had Ada not nudged Albert the Union sharply in the ribs, one of his old rugby songs might have desecrated the Edwards Brothers' coach.

The next big summer event was not one organised by Bethel Chapel, but it was one that everybody attended: the County Show in Newbridge. It ran for four days, and Elijah was glad that no funerals were planned, and that he would be able to go to the show on at least one day. And so he did.

The Showground was a hive of activity. There were tents and marquees as far as the eye could see. The St John Ambulance Association had the tent nearest to the gate. Its healing ministry was presided over by none other than Mrs Rachel Morris, resplendent in her uniform.

'There's an encouragement not to have an accident,' muttered Albert the Union to Ada as they walked past.

But it could be guaranteed that by the end of the Show a number of visitors would have fainted if the weather was hot; or slipped on the sodden field and twisted an ankle if the rains descended. And there was that famous occasion when the Mayor of Newbridge was nipped on the ankle by a dog. It became headline news in the *Sentinel*: NEWBRIDGE MAYOR SAVAGED BY A CHIHUAHUA.

There were tents where refreshments were sold; tents bursting with boots, wellingtons and agricultural clothing; tents full of new and second-hand bits of agricultural machinery; and a tent with more books on farming and country life than Elijah had ever seen in his life.

Various societies had their tents too. Elijah was especially interested in the tent sponsored by The British Goat Society. Since 1879 that august body had been championing the oft-despised goat. There was a table full of booklets and pamphlets on every aspect of goat keeping: how to show your goat; what to do when you goat is ill; the benefits of goats milk for children; and something about something called *caprine coccidiosis*. There were milk recording cards and books, the Society's *Journal*, and goat keepers' badges. There were posters advertising forthcoming goat shows, and there were pens in which a variety of show goats were on display: British Alpines, Anglo-Nubians with their floppy ears, Saanens with their beautiful white coats, and others. Goaty people from far and wide were chattering away about show judges to be particularly feared, the latest ear-marking tool, and such deliverances from experts in goat psychology as that goats are not to be thought of as if they were naughty children, for everything they do is done of set purpose.

Parts of the field were roped off for special exhibitions. In one area there was an exhibition of classic tractors. There in all their glory were a 1930 Massey-Harris – a four-wheel drive pioneer; a Model Fordson from 1933 – the first year in which they were manufactured in England; there were hay rakes, early combine harvesters, ploughs and much else besides. At one end of the enclosure some old-time harvesting was being demonstrated. An Aveling and Porter traction engine and threshing machine were hard at work. As might be expected, Albert the Union was there. He seemed to know all the steam enthusiasts for miles around, and as Elijah came along he told him more of the history of the Aveling and Porter company than any human could have absorbed in one go.

A little farther along Elijah came to an exhibition of rare breeds. He saw some Middle White and Gloucestershire Old Spot pigs, and the oldest breed of British cattle, the White Park. There were also Traditional Herefords and Lincoln Reds. He was particularly pleased to see some Welsh Balwen sheep, for during the dreadful storms of 1947 their numbers had been reduced to one flock, and one ram only had survived. But there they were, small and sprightly, with their black bodies, white feet and tails, and blazes of white across their faces.

In the centre of the field was a large roped-off area in which shows and entertainments of various kinds took place. At their appointed time the Newbridge Town Band gave an hour-long performance. As well as such stand-bys as Sousa marches and *Merry Widow* excerpts, they entered into the spirit of things by playing as many items with a farming theme as they could find: 'The Farmer's Boy', 'The Lincolnshire Poacher', and many more besides.

At the far end of the field was a recruiting tent for the armed services.

Each year one branch of the forces was responsible for manning the exhibition, and this time it was the turn of the Royal Air Force. Those responsible always brought along something to attract the crowds to their tent, and on this occasion the Air Force a fine example of a Hawker Hurricane fighter was on display. As Elijah was viewing the plane, who should come along but Ron and Glenys MacDonald.

'Ah!' said Ron, 'my favourite plane.' And he proceeded to tell Elijah that the Hurricane had first been mooted by the designer Sydney Camm in 1933, but the British Air Ministry had qualms about the monoplane structure. Their fears were allayed, however, 600 planes were ordered, and the Hurricane finally entered service in 1937. When the Battle of Britain began on 8 August 1940 thirty-two squadrons of Hurricanes were ready for action.

'They were so important,' said Ron, 'that more and more were needed. They were produced in various countries, and in Canada the Canadian Car and Foundry Company had their first one ready to fly on 9 January 1940.'

'Were the Canadian and British Hurricanes identical in all respects?' asked Elijah.

'They looked the same from the outside,' said Ron, 'but Canadian equipment was installed inside ours.'

At that moment a voice over the loudspeaker announced the start of the Dog Show, and Glenys was especially interested in that, so they went over to the main ring. County dog shows in Wales were not entirely on a par with Crufts. For one thing there was a preponderance of sheep dogs, and for another, there was a class for mongrels. Both the mongrels and the sheep dogs seemed unused to the degree of grooming they were receiving, while a Pekingese under the comb and brush wore a lofty yet slightly bored expression which clearly indicated that in the dog's mind it was simply being treated in the manner to which it was not only accustomed, but entitled. Elijah was very pleased that the winner of the terrier class was a member of a Welsh breed, a Sealyham named Sophie.

'What a lovely white coat she has,' said Elijah, 'and how friendly she looks.'

'Yes,' Glenys agreed. 'They really are a delightful breed. Captain John Edwardes of Haverfordwest did a good thing over a century and a half ago when he crossed Bull Terriers and West Highland Whites with Welsh Corgis to produce his perfect terrier.'

With impeccable timing, the show dogs no longer needing to stand for inspection like statues, some shots rang out from the adjacent field as the Down the Line version of clay pigeon shooting got under way. Elijah went across to watch some of it. There were the usual five competitors, who moved in turn along the five shooting stands. They were obviously keen on their sport, for Elijah noticed that they all had guns with over-and-under barrels – by far the most suitable for the task in hand. They were good at it too: very few clay targets escaped unscathed.

On leaving the shooting, Elijah returned to the central ring, where the Bampton Morris dancers were about to start their performance. The six dancers were dressed in their traditional white shirts, trousers and waist-coats, with ribbons on their bowler hats, and bells and ribbons below their knees. There was also the 'fool', carrying a pig's bladder and a cake stuck on a sword. They were accompanied by a fiddler and a melodeon player. It was all very colourful and boisterous, and the crowd clearly loved it. The dances were traditional to the Cotswold area, and included jigs, hand-kerchief and stick dances, and dances including much hand clapping.

By now it was late afternoon, and Elijah was feeling hungry. He went to one of the refreshment tents and bought a Cornish pasty, some Welsh cakes, and tea. Although he had not yet been in the area for a year, already he could recognise many faces and, indeed, some of his church members. 'If I sat here throughout the whole event,' he thought, 'I could do all my pastoral visiting without moving an inch.' One by one they came and greeted him, asking him what he had enjoyed most. This question – innocent enough when addressed to members of any other calling than Elijah's – had to be answered with a certain amount of pastoral tact. Unless he wanted to have his ear chewed off, it would have been no good telling Elwyn the pacifist that he had most enjoyed seeing the Hurricane. And Meirion would not have been at all impressed if he had nominated the Cotswold Morris Men as his favourites – 'Pagan cavortings' would have been Meirion's denunciatory judgement. But he came through the inquisition unscathed, and then went out for the final performance of the day, which was going to be a real treat, he was sure.

Elijah, we recall, had catholic tastes in music, but in certain moods he was particularly partial to traditional jazz. Imagine his delight, therefore, when he discovered that the closing concert of the day – thoughtfully timed to catch young people after work – was to be given by Alex Welsh and his Band. This was one of his favourite Chicago-style bands, and Alex Welsh was one of the most highly respected practitioners of his art. A large crowd had gathered, and a spontaneous cheer went up as the band set off with 'Dippermouth Blues'. Among many other items they played 'Lazy River', 'Georgia', and 'Please don't talk about me when I'm gone'. But Elijah was almost hopping for joy when they played 'Dapper Dan'. For this was the piece in which the famous and irrepressible drummer, Lennie Hastings, came into his own. He had only recently joined the Welsh band, but already he had made himself well at home. Sometimes he would put on a German soldier's helmet, fix a half-crown in one eye like a monacle, and sing in broken English after the style of Richard Tauber. But on this occasion he contented himself with a virtuoso drum solo, towards the end of which he paused for a bar whilst he hollered in animal fashion, 'OOh-ya! OOh-ya!' and received thunderous applause. At the end of the concert the encores were so many, and so generously supplied by Alex Welsh, that Elijah almost missed the last bus home. 'What a day it has been,' he thought. And then he thought, 'Tomorrow I must get ready for next Sunday.'

On the following Sunday another local custom fell to be observed: the Annual Life Boat Service. This was always held on the beach by the lifeboat station, and it was attended by locals and visitors alike. Not, indeed, that all the Christians of Bethel attended. The Reverend Calvin Rowlands, Horeb, kept his Baptists imprisoned in their chapel (though Hetty Bevan always played truant because in his younger days her late husband, Gwilym, had been a volunteer crew member, and her son Roland still was one); and the Rector was often elsewhere, and when he wasn't he would deign to read the Bible lesson or say the Blessing at the end. But he would never preach on the beach lest anyone might mistake him for a Wesleyan evangelist – something that would have required a considerable imagination. So it fell to Elijah to conduct the service and give the address.

Familiar themes were the Psalmist's, concerning those who go down to the sea in ships, and the story of Jesus's stilling of the storm.

On this occasion a large crowd had gathered, and the lifeboat crew were there in full strength. The Salvation Army Band from Newbridge had come along to accompany the singing. They always began with 'Eternal Father, strong to save', and this year was no exception. Then Elijah said a prayer and Roland Bevan read the Bible. Elijah then called upon Eryl Walters, the coxswain, to report on the year's activities with special reference to pastoral concerns. The assembled company learned that Jack Jones had sprained his wrist on one call-out, but there had been no fatalities. There followed a prayer for all those involved in the rescue service, and their families, and then Elijah invited the Newtown-on-Sea Fishermen's Choir to sing. This male voice choir, all of whose members were in Guernsey sweaters, was well known in the area. They sang a number of hymns with a nautical flavour, among them, 'Jesus, Saviour, pilot me', and 'Will your anchor hold?' Then Elijah addressed the crowd, an offering for the Royal National Lifeboat Institution was taken, and the final hymn, 'Now thank we all our God', was sung. Elijah pronounced the Benediction, and the crowd gradually dispersed.

By now the holiday season was in full swing, and Elijah wondered whether any of the visitors would make their way to a service at Bethel during their stay in the area. He knew that at least one of his members would not give any visitors a very warm welcome. For at the July Church Meeting the question had been raised, 'What are we to do about the visitors?' had been raised.

'Keep them out!' said Jeremiah Parry grumpily. Jeremiah was a farmer of an unusually crusty disposition. He had a particular 'down' on the English, not because he was an ardent Welsh Nationalist – there wasn't much of that in those days – but because he was convinced that any litter found in the area, and any of his field gates left open, were the sole responsibility of the English. In fact, something approaching fifty per cent of these tragedies were directly attributable to the Walters twins. Nevertheless, Jeremiah was opposed to the English.

'Just think of all the water they steal from Welsh hills without any payment,' he moaned.

'But they could say that if they didn't take the water Welsh fields would be even more waterlogged than they often are,' was Jenkin Jones's rejoinder.

Unconvinced, Jeremiah waged a silent war on visitors. He turned footpath signs around so that they would get lost; he put his prize bull in the big field through which a public footpath ran; and at a later point in the Church Meeting he took advantage of something Jenkin Jones said: 'If visitors are to come, we ought to make ourselves as presentable and welcoming as possible, so let's get the chapel notice board repainted.'

'I'll do it!' said Jeremiah, and everyone wondered what had got into him, for volunteering was not his usual style. But the wily one thought that if he repainted the board he could make the chapel's name and the minister's name so big that there would not be room to proclaim the times of the services. 'That'll fox the English,' he thought.

Jeremiah had had a certain amount of support at the meeting. Maldwyn Llewellyn made one of his rare interventions. The husband of Mrs Blodwen Llewellyn, LRAM, he was of necessity the strong and silent type. 'It's not that I dislike the English as such,' he said, 'but I fear that too many ramblers around here will erode the soil – look what's happening to Snowdon.'

'Drat it, Maldwyn,' expostulated Dai Cashbox, 'your Ossie does more harm to the fields with his motorbike scrambling than a whole army of ramblers.' And Maldwyn, unable to disagree, subsided into the silence which was his wont.

'What's more,' piped up Mrs Rachel Morris, 'what would your Blodwen say if she thought you were keeping visitors at bay when she's all set to sell them cream teas between piano lessons?'

They did not need to speculate on what Blodwen would say, for she was there. 'I'd wring his neck,' she said, whereupon a look of terror flitted across Maldwyn's face.

'We must be hospitable, it's only Christian,' said Reginald Phillips.

'With a B&B and three caravans, you've got to say that,' muttered Jeremiah Parry.

By now Elijah had had enough of this, so he shamed them with piety: 'Is there anyone here who thinks the arguments against visitors we've heard here tonight are more important than our God-given obligation to proclaim the Good News of Jesus Christ to all who pass our way?'

That was what Elijah's Classics professor would have called a question expecting the answer no. It evoked silence. Not even Jeremiah Parry could bring himself to answer 'Yes'; and he even began to think that perhaps, after all, it would be petty and spiteful not to put the times of services on the notice board.

'We must give the visitors refreshments if they come,' said Rachel Morris; and this was agreed.

'And we need to appoint someone to greet them warmly in the vestibule when they arrive,' said Elijah.

'I nominate Jeremiah Parry,' said Albert the Union, wickedly.

'I'll do it!' said Jeremiah.

'That's about the quickest conversion we've ever had at Bethel,' thought Meirion.

'Would you like the responsibility of buying a Visitors Book?' Elijah asked Dai Cashbox, thinking that if he made it an honour to obtain the book, Dai would not be so likely to quibble about the price.

'As good as done,' said Dai. 'I'll ask Betty to get one in town.'

In the event, there had been a trickle of visitors to Bethel during the first four Sundays of August, and refreshments had duly been provided for them and the locals in Roderick Hall. Of course, Ron and Glenys MacDonald were visitors, but they were fifty per cent Bethel anyway. But others were English, and Jeremiah Parry, true to his word, forced himself to smile at them and give them hymn books.

On the last Sunday of the month there was a veritable avalanche of ramblers – more than a dozen of them. To judge from the colour of their faces, they were in the pink of condition; and they were in very good spirits. They came from Cockermouth, and most Saturdays would find them on one of the Lake District peaks. But once a year they all went on a rambling holiday together, and this year, here they were at Bethel. Their leader, one Doris, was of the kind found on many a footpath. Not to put too fine a point on it, she was sturdy; her dimpled knees found their way, not without some difficulty, through the legs of her shorts. Her freckled face was topped by ginger hair so bright that it was as effective as any of those coloured hats that circumspect ramblers wear in case they have an accident and need to be spotted by a helicopter. She had a rucksack on her back in which she carried what seemed to be provisions for a fortnight; her pockets bulged with maps, a compass, and a tin of first aid products. Meirion was particularly impressed to see a Bible and a concordance struggling to escape from her upper chest pocket. All of the ramblers had badges sewn to their rucksacks, bearing such slogans as 'Jesus saves'.

At the door Doris nearly shook Jeremiah Parry's hand off: he felt the pain for some days afterwards. 'Greetings, brother,' she boomed, 'I'm Doris Posslit.' Jeremiah was familiar enough with the name 'Doris', but Posslit was a name he had never heard before. He was so taken aback that he could hardly remember his own name.

'I'm Mr Jeremiah Parry,' he said, rather formally. He gave her a hymn book and then asked her whether she would like to sign the Visitors Book.

'Yes, yes,' she clucked; and with that she spun around in the direction of the book, her rucksack sending Jeremiah's neat pile of hymn books flying.

'Thou gurt gammerstang! Fat's in t' fire noo,' said her husband, Dick.

Jeremiah had never heard such words, but he gathered that Doris was not being complimented.

'What's ta mekkin' that flaysome din fer, Doris?' asked her brother-in-law, Caleb, cheekily.

Undeterred, Doris wrote her name carefully in the Visitors Book: Doris Postlethwaite.

'Well!' Jeremiah thought to himself as he read it. 'So that's how you spell Posslit: I thought she took a time over it.'

The rest of the ramblers signed the book – there were Capsticks, Woofs, Sedgwicks Milburns and Tysons ('None of those names here in Bethel village,' mused Jeremiah) – and then they all trooped into the chapel. They sang lustily, and Elijah had never had a sermon so frequently punctuated by 'Amen'. Doris even managed two 'Praise be's and one 'Alleluia!'

Afterwards they all adjourned to Roderick Hall and enjoyed the refreshments. Jenkin Jones made a beeline for Noah Capstick, who had given a farm address in the Visitors Book, and they had a long chat about milk yields, as farmers do. Elijah found himself talking to Bobby Milburn, who asked him, 'What goes on around here in the way of sport?'

Elijah told him of the clay pigeon shooting, the hunt, and the fishing.

'Have you ever heard of hound trailing?' asked Bobby.

'No,' said Elijah – but he was soon to hear about it at great length.

Bobby was a great follower of hound trailing, that Cumbrian race in which hounds follow an aniseed and paraffin trail over the fells.

'It's very exciting,' said Bobby, 'and nothing gets killed – that's the best part of it.'

'Do the hounds enjoy it?' asked Elijah.

'Oh yes,' Bobby replied. 'They get a slap-up meal including glucose, the whites of eggs and beef, and then nothing for the twenty-four hours before the race. Then they race, and then they have a good feed again.'

'Do the hounds do any special training?'

'Yes. They are walked four hours in a morning and four hours in the evening over fell country. If the dogs are not fit, the walkers are! One of the most famous trainers today is Joe Mather of Cleator Moor.'

'I suppose that during a race the hounds are out of sight for most of the time?'

'That's right,' said Bobby. 'That's why every dog is marked before it sets off so that no rascals can substitute another, fresh, dog halfway round. There are a few crooks in every sport. The only thing I don't like about it is the gambling. It goes against my religion. I think you can have good fun without that!'

'How long are the trails,' Elijah asked.

'Well, for dogs over two years – nine or ten miles; but for puppies, four or five. It can take a hound anything from twenty minutes to three-quarters of an hour to cover a ten-mile trail, depending on the fitness of the hound and the difficulty of the terrain.'

'How many places hold hound trails?'

'Too many to count,' said Billy. 'Last season there were 724 trails during the season – that's 154 more than in the previous year. There was a bit of a mix-up at the Dog Produce meeting at Shap, when the trailers didn't do a very good job, and the scent for one race got blown by the wind to the dogs in another race, and that put them off their trail. The senior champion last year was a dog called Wingate, and the champion puppy was Lonning Lad.'

Elijah felt he had learned a lot from this genuine enthusiast, but by now it was time for the ramblers to leave, and for the Bethel members to return to their homes. They bade one another fond farewells, and the ramblers walked down the road singing 'I am H-A-P-P-Y.'

At the September Church Meeting Dai Cashbox gave the longest financial report that anyone could remember. As compared with his usual, 'All's OK', he was positively verbose. 'The offerings for the first four Sundays of August averaged £21/40/5 per week,' he said. 'The offering on the last Sunday of the month amounted to £63/8/6.'

'So those visitors gave as hard as they sang and listened,' said Jenkin Jones.

'Let's see what we can do to attract more visitors next summer,' enthused Dai Cashbox.

'They fairly put us to shame,' said Meirion, mournfully. 'They must all tithe like the Bible says.'

The following Sunday Elijah preached with great conviction on 2 Corinthians 9:7, 'God loveth a cheerful giver.'

10

The Reverend Elijah Morgan
Takes a Wife

The telephone rang in Elijah Morgan's study. He was halfway through his sermon for the following Sunday, and he had a problem. His theme was the ascension of Christ, and Elijah was haunted by some New Testament lectures he had heard from the delightfully intitialled Professor Francis Algernon Gervase Ash. Fag Ash had become a disciple of the German scholar, Rudolf Bultmann, and Bultmann was famed for his determination to 'demythologise' the New Testament.

'We cannot any longer believe in a three-tiered universe, with heaven above, the earth where we are, and hell below,' thundered Ash. 'Accordingly, we must delve behind the old imagery and find contemporary ways of communicating the *meaning* of the old text to twentieth-century Christians.'

The effect of this statement was electric. So electric, indeed, that some of Elijah's more conservative classmates immediately called for a prayer meeting at 6.00 a.m. the next morning to pray for the Professor's soul. Even Principal Morgan MacDonald, who heard about the affair later in the day, quaked a little – not so much because he feared that his colleague's soul was at risk, as because he could think of a number of churches from which the flow of funds to the College would cease if word got out that the authorities there had taken an unduly liberal turn.

Elijah declined the invitation to attend the prayer meeting. Being of a balanced, studious disposition, he knew that he risked being viewed askance by some of his friends; indeed at the time he had that creepy feeling that accompanies the suspicion that one is being 'prayed for' by the ultra godly at some unearthly hour in the morning. What he was now experiencing was the difficulty Fag had left him with of preaching about the ascension without making any spatial references whatsoever!

He picked up the telephone and a man's voice said, 'I've been living with my girl friend for the last six years, and I think it's time I made an honest woman of her. Will you marry us?'

Two thoughts immediately crossed Elijah's mind. First, this was a more than ordinarily direct approach, not at all in keeping with the normal manner of the village folk all around him. Secondly, who on earth could it be? Surely he would have known of anyone in this position; it would be the talk of the village; and it wasn't. So he decided to play for time.

'What is you name?'

'Oliver Cromwell.'

Now Elijah really smelled a rat – and he thought he recognised the chuckle that accompanied the name. 'Goronwy,' he blurted out, 'it's you!'

'So it is!' replied the Reverend Goronwy Jenkins, minister to a group of four ailing churches on the opposite side of the county.

Goronwy had been in Elijah's year in College. They were different in every way, but very good friends. Goronwy was a couple of years older than Elijah At the age of sixteen he had gone straight into the building trade. He was tall and strong, with a shock of unruly, curly, black hair: the kind of person whose suit would never quite fit, even if it were made to measure. Elijah, as we know, was of medium height, slight of build and tidy in appearance. Where Elijah was studious, Goronwy found book-work tedious; he scraped through the Diploma in Theology by the skin of his teeth and the generosity of Professor Ash, who would have done anything not to have to push a reluctant Goronwy through Nunn's *Elements of New Testament Greek* one more time.

Both Elijah and Goronwy had a sense of humour, but whereas Elijah's was of the quiet, wry kind, Goronwy was the slapstick merchant, the practical joker. It was he who had masterminded the kidnapping of John Wesley's bust from the Methodist College. It was he who, following defeat by the Baptists on the football field, brought his roofing skills to bear by scaling the 'water babies'' College walls and visiting every chimney pot on the treacherous roof with a view to covering it with a slate, thereby smoking out the saints below. By the time the front door of the Baptist edifice was thrown open and the students came coughing out, Goronwy and his pals had taken cover in the safety of the shrubbery surrounding the spacious front lawn. The final touch was best of all. As the Baptists made their hasty exit, their eyes streaming, their noses running, they were confronted by a large poster on which 'Inky' Meredith, a Congregationalist student whose hobby was calligraphy, had turned to the prophet Isaiah's vision and written in large, beautiful, characters, ISAIAH vi:4. Even the Baptists, thought Inky, would know that reference: 'The whole house was filled with smoke.' Now here was Goronwy on the end of the line.

'The Lord has put it into my heart to make contact with you,' he 'piously' began – whereupon Elijah, remembering that Goronwy had never been near the godlier type of prayer meetings, burst out, 'Come off it; what do you want?'

'No, really,' said Goronwy, 'I am pastorally concerned about you.'

'Why?' asked Elijah, quite unaware that he was in any particular pastoral need.

'Because I hear that those rascals at Bethel are running you into the ground. You need a break. Take a day off. Do something completely different.'

Elijah reflected that it was undeniable that he had been working very hard. Before he had accepted the call to Bethel the deacons had assured him that he would be free to take every Monday off. It seldom worked. Monday seemed to be a great day for funerals, ministers' fraternals, and pastoral tragedies of diverse kinds.

'Meet me tomorrow morning at 10.00 a.m.,' ordered Goronwy in tones which booked no opposition.

'Where?' asked Elijah.

'At the tea shop opposite the Central Library in Westford.'

'Why there?' asked Elijah.

'Because Westford is halfway between your place and mine, and it's two towns away from where either of us lives,' replied Goronwy. Elijah could not fault Goronwy's geography, but the significance of the last part of his reply did not dawn upon him until much later.

'I'll be there,' said Elijah; he put the phone down, and returned to the ascension.

Early next morning Elijah hitched a lift with Rachel and Bill Morris, who were going to the cattle market in Newbridge, and from there he just managed to catch the Westford train. He had never been to Westford before. Like Newbridge, Westford was an old market town, but much larger. Unlike Newbridge there was coal beneath, and the outskirts of the mining industry were there. There was also a large public school which attracted wealthier students from all over Wales, and some from beyond. The resulting mixture of farmers, miners, schoolmasters and their wives, traders and professional people made for a diverse community.

It was not difficult to find the Library. A beneficiary of Carnegie money, it occupied a prominent site in the centre of town. Directly opposite was the tea shop, and there, grinning at the window table, was Goronwy. They ordered tea and scones; they reminisced about College days; they shared their early experiences of pastoral ministry. Elijah was just thinking that Goronwy was making rather frequent references to Elijah's need to 'get out of himself', when Goronwy glanced at his watch and said, 'Come on, we must hurry!'

'Where are we going?' asked Elijah, puzzled.

'You'll see, it's just around the corner.'

And just around the corner it was: the Locarno Ballroom. In went Goronwy, with Elijah trailing after him, bemused. He had never been in such a place. He could think of certain members of his family, not to mention certain members of the Bethel diaconate, who would be horrified to the point of apoplexy if they ever found out that he had been in the Westford Locarno. The strategic significance of the fact that the Locarno was two towns away from both his and Goronwy's pastorate began to dawn upon him.

Up the wide, thick-carpeted, stairs they went, and Goronwy flung open the door at the top. The vast floor, the stage, the lights – all were there, but the place was entirely empty. 'Of course,' thought Elijah to himself, 'nobody dances at 11.30 a.m. on a Thursday,' and he began to feel a little safer. Just then the door by the side of the stage opened, and in came a woman. She did not so much walk as glide. She was a vision of loveliness. Elijah had never seen anyone so beautiful. She had long flame-red hair, green eyes, and a delightful smile. She was about five-foot-five in height, and, Elijah guessed, about twenty-four years of age.

'Good morning, Mr Jenkins,' she said. Here voice was warm yet business-like. 'Have you brought me another student?'

'Not exactly,' said Goronwy, 'he's just come along to watch.' And Goronwy introduced Elijah to Miss Gordon, explaining, 'She's my teacher.'

Elijah was astounded. He knew that Goronwy was game for most things, but the thought of this six foot, sturdy ex-builder gliding sylph-like around a ballroom floor boggled his imagination. Elijah sat on a chair at the side of the room. In his own person he constituted the entire audience.

Miss Gordon walked towards the gramophone on the stage, and as she went Goronwy grinned at Elijah and said, 'It's great exercise, boyo; I come every week; and if I play my cards right I might win a bronze medal in a year or so.'

'It's not so much a question of cards as feet,' said Miss Gordon briskly. 'Shall we begin?'

She pressed the switch on the gramophone and out came the unmistakable voice of Victor Silvester: 'One, two, one-two-three ...' and he was off into 'You're dancing on my heart'. As Elijah watched the proceedings he thought that the substitution of 'feet' for 'heart' would not be inappropriate, for Goronwy's size elevens posed a significant threat to Miss Gordon, and Elijah felt strangely protective of her. She was, however, more than able to take care of herself. Already an Associate of the Imperial Society of Teachers of Dancing, she was well up in the tricks of her trade. She reached up, held Goronwy's shoulders and manoeuvered him around the room. She watched his feet intently; Goronwy watched his feet intently; and Elijah watched Miss Gordon intently.

All too soon Goronwy's half-hour was up. He looked at his watch. 'Must dash,' he said, 'got a funeral at 2.00.' And off he went. Elijah and Miss Gordon were left looking at each other.

'Would you like a lesson?' she asked.

'Oh no – thank you,' stammered Elijah, 'But I'd love to take you to lunch.' He thought those last words were just in his head, but quite involuntarily they tumbled out of his mouth. He couldn't believe that he'd said that. Still less could he believe that Miss Gordon accepted the invitation.

So off they went together. Thus began a sincere, ministerially prudent, courtship.

When at last Elijah reached home he was in even more difficulties with the ascension of Christ than he was before he had set out. His mind wandered from Bultmann to Fag Ash, to Goronwy, to Victor Silvester, but above all to Miss Gordon, whose name, he had by now discovered, was Felicity. So flustered was he that at one point he inadvertently knocked his Bible off the desk and it fell to the floor, open at the Song of Songs, those moving, ancient, love poems which, Elijah recalled, had been recited in class by the aptly named Old Testament Professor Moses Isaac, in an ardour-damping monotone which could only have been achieved by one immersed for years in the desiccated world of Hebrew philology.

At last the ascension sermon was done, and on Sunday it was preached. Not a single spatial reference. Bultmann would have been proud of Elijah. 'The ascension,' he declared, 'means that Christ is with us *now*.' But Elijah's homiletic strategy was rumbled by the godly deacon, Meirion Hughes. He was an avid reader of the weekly paper, *The Christian*, and a faithful user of the Scripture Union daily Bible notes. As he passed Elijah on the way out he prodded him in the chest with the words, 'But our Lord *did* go UP!'

Somewhat mortified, Elijah returned home to the Manse. No sooner had he prepared his sausages for frying than the telephone rang. It was Dr Iorwerth Lewis of Newbridge. 'I am speaking in my new capacity of County Union Secretary, Idris Llewellyn having retired,' the learned man began. 'The next meeting will take place at Ebenezer, Westford, a week next Wednesday, and I should like you to offer the opening prayer. We begin at 2.30 prompt.' Elijah said that he would be honoured to accept the invitation.

Was it Providence? Elijah thought it might be. His conviction in the matter was sufficiently strong for him to phone Felicity. He had to come to Westford on official business a week next Wednesday. Was it possible that she could meet him at some time for a cup of tea? She seemed quite pleased at the prospect, but explained that her only free time was 3.30 p.m. 'Excellent,' said Elijah, 'I'll see you at the tea room.' In accepting her time Elijah had swiftly calculated that the 2.30 prompt meeting would begin at 2.40; that there would be a hymn, his prayer, a welcome from the chairman, and the famously long list of apologies; then by 3.25 the Lord's representatives would be well into an argument about something or other, and Elijah would be able to slip out unnoticed. And so it was.

After a most enjoyable meeting with Felicity, Elijah scuttled back to Ebenezer in time for tea. He greeted his acquaintances in a rather mechanical manner; his thoughts were elsewhere. After tea there was to be a missionary meeting with slides. The speaker was the bun-haired, bespectacled, Miss Elspeth McIntyre who for the past thirty years had been fixing splints here, delivering babies there, all over the more remote parts of Rhodesia. Of muscular build, and with a distinct tendency to swashbuckle, she had in her school days been captain of lacrosse. Her gusto in rallying her troops in that cause stood her in good stead now. Reputed to be able to give successive patients bed baths at the rate of fifteen per hour, she was clearly not a person to be trifled with – and never had been. Dr Iorwerth Lewis introduced her and she began to enthuse about the remarkable work the Lord was doing in Rhodesia, aided by herself. After about ten minutes she issued the command, 'Lights out!' and out they went. And out, too, went Elijah. He had been sitting in the back row by the door, and before you could say 'London Missionary Society' he was gone.

He walked briskly through the narrow downtown streets, round a corner, and there it was: the Locarno. Brightly illuminated, it looked even grander than it had earlier in the day. It was plastered with special posters announcing the visit that week of the famous Lew Stone and his band. This was a real treat for the Locarno's cliente, made possible by the fact that the Locarno belonged to the huge Mecca circuit of dance halls, and the company could post even its top London bands to the provinces at a whim. So there in Westford was Lew Stone of broadcasting fame.

Up the plush stairs Elijah went, and then up again to the balcony from which vantage point non-dancers could view the proceedings. The nearer he got, the louder the music became. Not indeed that Lew Stone blasted the dancers off the floor as some of his peers did. His style was thoughtful, rhythmic, and attuned to the needs of the dancers. As Elijah reached his balcony seat the band was playing 'Anything goes' and the dancers below were clearly enjoying it. The place was packed. 'Far more than I get to prayer meeting,' thought Elijah, ruefully. He thoroughly enjoyed the music. Felicity later told him that Lew Stone was one of the most imaginative arrangers in the business and had, indeed, written the standard work on harmony and arranging for dance bands.

The rules at the Locarno, as at all the other Mecca dance halls, were strict. No smoking on the dance floor; no alcoholic beverages anywhere in the building. There was, however, lemonade by the gallon, and it was served on the balcony. The lively quickstep came to an end, and Lew Stone turned to the microphone. In his quiet, unassuming Cockney voice he said, 'This brings us to the end of the first session, ladies and gentlemen. Will you now please welcome Ivor Jones and his sextet.' With that he struck up the slow waltz, 'Lovely lady', and Elijah had the surprise of his life – or, at any rate, the first surprise of that evening. The stage began to revolve, with Lew Stone and his band going off to Elijah's left and Ivor Jones's sextet coming round on his right – all of them playing 'Lovely lady'. Elijah had no idea that exactly the same revolution took place to exactly the same tune in the larger Meccas up and down the land.

The sextet was made up of competent local musicians, all of them part-time. They kept things going while the main band had their refreshments. Ivor Jones himself owned the busiest butcher's shop in town. When standing in front of his sextet he brought his baton down with as much precision, and with nearly as much force, as his axe on the several carcasses he butchered each day. The waltz ended, a quickstep followed, and then came the most difficult ballroom dance of all, the slow foxtrot. Ivor launched into 'If I didn't care' and the dancers did their best. At the end of it Ivor turned to the microphone and said, 'At this point we come to our regular "Improve your Dancing" slot.' Then came Elijah's second big surprise of the evening. Ivor continued, 'Tonight we shall focus on the foxtrot, and here to teach us the Hover Feather variation is our very own Miss Felicity Gordon.' The sextet broke into a snappy fanfare, the crowd applauded, Felicity came onto the stage, and Elijah nearly fell over the balcony rail in astonishment.

Felicity handled the eager horde with ease. She communicated enthusiasm, she effortlessly kept order. She demonstrated the eight steps of the variation, performed them with her most advanced pupil, and walked the dancers through them. 'We're ready now,' she said to Ivor, whereupon he played the foxtrot again so that the variation could be practised. Felicity and her pupil homed in on couples in difficulty, and in the end all seemed pleased with their new accomplishment. At the last chord Ivor called Felicity to the platform, thanked her profusely, everyone applauded again, she curtseyed and walked off; but not before she had caught sight of Elijah. She made a beeline for the balcony and Elijah proposed to her over a mug of Mecca lemonade, and she accepted him.

The mission in Rhodesia would have to wait for Elijah's attention. There was no room in his head for it tonight. He did not even return to Ebenezer. Instead he walked Felicity home and then went straight to the station. He arrived just as the last train was about to leave. He hurried aboard. On arriving at Newbridge, Edwards Brothers the bus company by now being in bed, he was faced by a seven-mile walk back to his Manse. Never had a seven-mile walk seemed so effortless to him.

Two or three days later the telephone rang in the Manse. It was Dr Emlyn Matthias of Salem, Westford. His doctorate was different in kind from that of Dr Iorwerth Lewis, the scholar. Dr Matthias's was of the honorary variety, and from a small American college at that. He was renowned as a preacher; his was a household name throughout Wales, and his fame had spread across the Atlantic. His sermons were widely known and loved. People from Holyhead to Newport and from Flint to St David's had been reduced to tears by his highly elaborated (and textually unsupported) account of Jairus's daughter. And some of the congregations to whom he had preached felt as if they knew every stone in the mountains around Zion. A number of his ministerial colleagues took him with a pinch of salt. His college contemporaries recalled his inability to pass even the Diploma; the antennae of the textual analysts among them were quick to pick up the slightest hint of one of Spurgeon's sermons issuing from the Doctor's mouth. But all, young and old, liberal and conservative, agreed that no one could weep as effectively as he in the pulpit.

In a voice dripping with unction and replete with decibels Dr Matthias boomed down the telephone line: 'Mr Morgan, my fine young brother. How impressed I was by your prayer at the County Union meeting. It was so sincere; it was beautifully phrased; it glistened with godliness; it brought heaven close; the very angels rejoiced. What an inestimable privilege it would be for my people to hear your dulcet tones again! Will you come over to help us? [The Macedonian allusion was not lost on Elijah, BD]. I have been summoned to proclaim the Lord's Word in Rapid City, South Dakota [he announced the location with such emphasis that it might have been the centre of the homiletic universe – something which Elijah silently doubted], and I regard this as a divine call that I dare not refuse. [Elijah was quite ashamed of himself for thinking, 'You probably can't refuse a free trip and a fat fee either.'] May I cordially invite you to conduct the morning and evening services at Salem, in three weeks' time?'

Elijah was quite sure that he had never before received such an elegantly phrased (or was it merely a smooth?) invitation. He *said* he would be honoured to come; he *thought*, I shall be able to see Felicity! But, he pointed out, there were no trains until the afternoon on Sunday, so as he had no transport of his own he would not be able to come.

'Fear not!' boomed Dr Matthias with as much conviction as the angel to the Bethlehem shepherds, 'all is arranged. My deacon, Mr Griffith Thomas, MBE, will send his man over to you on Saturday afternoon. Be ready at three.'

So it turned out. Mr Griffith Thomas owned the largest shop in Westford. It was a department store where you could buy anything from a thimble to a bedroom suite. On the appointed Saturday Mr Thomas's 'man' drew up at the Manse in a shining Bentley – to much twitching of nearby curtains. He wore a peaked cap; he held the door for Elijah; and he delivered him in style to Mr and Mrs Pugh (no relation to Dai Cashbox), who were to be Elijah's hosts.

The Pughs were very hospitable. Their house was modest but comfortable – about ten minutes from the town centre. They served a scrumptious evening meal and afterwards Mrs Pugh said, 'What would you like to do for the rest of the evening, Mr Morgan?'

'Well,' said Elijah, 'what I usually do is to go for a walk to gather my thoughts for Sunday.' This was absolutely true. He would wander through the meadows and down to the rustic bridge over the stream, lean on the parapet and ponder. Of course, in Westford there were no meadows, no rustic bridge, no stream. But there was the Locarno.

In ten minutes he was there. Felicity gave her demonstration. They chatted over lemonade, and then Elijah felt he should hurry back to the Pughs. At the exit of the ballroom there stood a tall doorman in evening dress. As Elijah approached the man held out his right hand. Elijah extended his right hand as if to shake it, but the big man took Elijah's hand, turned it palm down, and stamped the back of it with the word 'Paid' in violet ink.

'What's that for?' asked Elijah.

'So you can get in again without paying when you come back from the pub,' said the man. And it dawned upon Elijah that this was the Mecca organisation's way of assisting those of its customers the slaking of whose thirst required more than a mug of lemonade. Elijah, of course, did not go to the pub. He went back to the Pughs and spent the rest of the evening in cheerful conversation with them, his right, branded, hand firmly stuffed in his pocket.

The next morning he stood in the pulpit at Salem, facing the largest congregation he had ever preached to. And there, under the rear gallery, almost behind a pillar, was Felicity. She was wearing a fashionable full poplin skirt and a short-sleeved blouse. On her head was a dainty hat. Elijah's heart leaped, and he preached as never before.

Meanwhile, back at Bethel, Jenkin Jones the secretary asked the deacons to forgather informally after the morning service. In the history of Bethel it had often transpired that these informal meetings were the ones at which the most important decisions were taken. They met on this occasion in the absence of their minister, but that was the point. Jenkin Jones said, 'I have called you together because Mr Meirion Hughes has something to say to us all.' And off the pious Meirion went:

'I am deeply grieved to bring you distressing tidings,' he began.

'Who has died?' they all wondered.

Meirion continued, 'As most of you know my second cousin twice removed is the proprietoress of Lovegrove's in Westford.' Beatrice Lovegrove was a pillar of the Brethren Assembly in Westford. Meirion sometimes envied her: the solemn and theologically conservative ways of the Brethren would have suited him quite well. But he could never quite sort out all the divine dispensations and, in any case, the Brethren had not penetrated Bethel village. Beatrice was, if anything more metaphorically strait-laced than Meirion and, in the most literal sense she devoted her working life to making others strait-laced too. For in her shop she specialised in ladies undergarments. It would be a gross untruth to say that her stock was at the height of fashion. It would be entirely true to say that the garments she sold were of industrial strength and ideally suited to the distributive tasks they were called upon to perform.

'Where is this leading?' the deacons all wondered.

'Lovegrove's is directly opposite the Locarno Ballroom,' said Meirion.

'We all know that,' they thought, 'why should this concern us?'

'And,' said Meirion in the most sepulchral tones, 'my second cousin twice removed has witnessed, from her shop window, with her own eyes, the Reverend Elijah Morgan coming down the steps of the Locarno hand in hand with the red-headed dancing *mistress.*'

Meirion's emphasis upon that last word gave it a most sinister ring. He began to stir up his indignation.

'We all know that dance halls are dens of vice. The Locarno is the Sodom and Gomorrah of Westford. Can we rest content that our minister should frequent such a place? Will not our consciences accuse us if we do not face him with his sin?'

'I don't see that it's any of our business,' said the flashily dressed Elwyn Roberts.

'We can count on you to say something radical and ungodly like that,' snorted Meirion, who had for some time suspected Elwyn of occasionally 'flinging a leg' in the modest palais above the Co-op in Newbridge.

Stirring the pot, Elwyn retorted, 'Dora Bryan met her husband in a dance hall in Oldham.' Before he was halfway through the sentence, however, he realised that this was no way to convince Meirion, for whom an up-and-coming comedy actress was little, if at all, better than a dancing teacher. Meirion looked at him with disdain. 'Why don't you stick to something wholesome, like Shakespeare?' he challenged. In the mind of Elwyn, who spent much of his time devising strategies for deflecting impressionable young people from the raunchier portions of the bard of

Avon's texts, an entire essay formed in response to his fellow deacon. But he decided not to bother.

Following in Elwyn's line, and as if offering the clinching argument, Dai Cashbox observed, 'I hear that Victor Silvester is the son of a Church of England parson.'

'There you are then,' said Albert 'Union' Williams, his sturdy Nonconformist principles damning Mecca and all its works in an instant.

But Dai's intervention put Meirion on the spot. Though pious and narrow, he was a man of integrity, and he knew that there was another side of the argument, for the famous band leader, Henry Hall, had come out of the Salvation Army. And had not Meirion himself bought Henry Hall's recording of 'The Teddy Bears Picnic' for his niece last Christmas? What a dilemma! Meirion could not endorse Albert's expostulation, but if he countered it he would be manifesting a knowledge of 'the world' which he, as a godly man, was not supposed to have. So he deflected the discussion on to the dancing teacher.

'Do we want our minister to be consorting with a Jezebel?' he asked, defiantly. Now Dai Cashbox's acquaintance with most of the Old Testament characters was slight to say the least, so the allusion to the wicked woman of the books of Kings was quite lost on him. 'A Jezebel,' Dai retorted, clearly supposing that the Jezebels were one of those new-fangled sects: 'I don't care if she's a Jehovah's Witness – can she bake?' Dai the treasurer was utterly persuaded (a) that a minister's wife who could bake was worth at least £3 per annum to the church, considering the Autumn Fayre, the bring and buy sales and suchlike; (b) that this additional income would balance the books; and (c) that if Mr Morgan secured such a wife Dai could postpone increasing his own weekly offerings for a while.

So it went on and on. Jenkin Jones, the wise secretary, knew how to keep his powder dry. At last, almost as if changing the subject entirely, he casually said, 'By the way, I received a letter yesterday, and I'd like to read it to you.' They quietened down, and Jenkin Jones read as follows:

Dear Mr Jones

How delighted my wife and I are to learn of the engagement of our daughter, Felicity, to your minister, the Reverend Elijah Morgan.

We propose to take a holiday in your area soon, and we very much look forward to meeting you and the members of your church.

With every good wish,

Yours sincerely,
Gervase Gordon,
Bishop of Godchester.

The silence was palpable. Nobody spoke for a while. Albert the Union was quite put out: 'Not only a Church of England dancing teacher, but gentry!' he thought to himself. The pious Meirion was utterly deflated. He had no words left: a dancing teacher, an Anglican, and English! As for Rachel Morris, all her hopes for her Shirley were dashed. Never would she grace the Manse as the minister's wife. All the none-too-subtle hints, all the engineered 'coincidental' meetings had been to no avail. For his part, Dai Cashbox gloomily reflected, 'I still don't know if she can bake.'

'I propose,' said Jenkin Jones, 'that we write a letter of congratulation to Mr Morgan and Miss Gordon, and that when he comes back from Westford tomorrow, we tell him he can have an extra day off.'

With varying degrees of enthusiasm, a unanimous result was achieved.

The wedding duly took place in Godchester Cathedral. Most of the Bethel folk could not attend: they were frail, or they could not get time off work, and it was a long way. But Jenkin Jones, a farmer able to call upon neighbours to watch over his animals, was there with Dilys. On his return he remarked, concise as ever, 'That was an *occasion!*' The *Newbridge Sentinel* made much more of it: 'LOCAL MINISTER WEDS,' shrieked the main headline on page one. The sub-heading was even more of a circulation-booster: 'From dance hall to cathedral'. Few ministers have found fame as quickly as did Elijah Morgan.

On returning to the Manse after their honeymoon, Mr and Mrs Morgan found, to their delight, that the larder was bursting with enough provisions to last for months, there were gifts on the tables – tea services, bed linen and the like; and there were seven sacks of potatoes in the shed.

Among the many cards received was one from the Reverend Goronwy Jenkins. Underneath the customary greeting the ebullient Goronwy had scrawled in his generous hand: 'I had to pay to get the bronze medal. You got the teacher for free. Want to swap?' Happily, none laughed more spontaneously than the new Mrs Morgan.

The new Mrs Morgan settled quickly into life at Bethel. She graciously declined the chair of the Young Wives' Club – well, they had been young in 1920, though she promised to teach them the jitterbug if they dared. She even prevailed upon the deacons to allow her to give dancing classes in Roderick Hall on Tuesdays, Thursdays and Saturday mornings. She presented this as a service to the whole community, there being no village hall. When she also made it clear that she would be *hiring* the hall, Dai Cashbox suddenly became a wholehearted enthusiast for all things terpsichorean. On Tuesdays Mrs Morgan would teach Old Tyme dancing, and the Bethel members (and a few Baptists who dared to face the wrath of the Reverend Calvin Rowlands, Horeb) soon became so graceful in the Velita and so martial in the Military Two-step that Harry Davidson himself would have been proud of them. The children made excellent progress in their tap dancing classes on Saturday mornings, though little Blodwen Parry never really mastered the snatch.

But the highlight of the week was the Thursday Square Dance. Even Meirion Hughes was won over to this, not so much on principle – in fact, he almost choked on his principles, but because Miss Shirley Morris had asked him to go with her to see what this new-fangled American craze was all about. They gathered in the hall, and just as Mrs Morgan was about to put on the first record, the door flung open, and in strode deacon and deputy head teacher Elwyn Roberts, making the kind of entrance that befitted a drama teacher. Silence descended upon them all – it could have been a Quaker meeting. For there was Elwyn *sans* winkle pickers, *sans* drainpipes, *sans* velvet-collared jacket. There was Elwyn in a ten gallon hat, neckerchief, bright Western shirt and jeans, and cowboy boots. Amidst the sartorially diverse and not-at-all-Western-looking company he looked quite out of place – but no more so than the lugubrious Meirion. Whereas the rest of the men had taken off their jackets and ties and undone their collars, there was Meirion in his customary black suit and high starched collar ('Always ready for the next funeral,' Jenkin Jones had one day quipped), and utterly persuaded that no one other than his intended (if it ever came to it) would see his Adam's apple.

The gramophone wound up, the record on, there they all were, learning the steps from Mrs Morgan and putting them into practice. Felicity
moved among them, rescuing them when they lost their sense of direction, and cheerfully encouraging the least technically competent. And
who should be serving as caller? None other than Albert the Union. He
was not one for dancing, having sustained a leg wound during the war
('Nothing wrong with his drinking elbow,' snarled righteous Meirion on
hearing this excuse). But calling was Albert's calling, so to speak. His
stentorian tones could easily be heard above the gramophone – indeed
they could have been hear above the Treorchy Male Voice Choir; and his
rhythmic orders were barked in such a manner as to brook no opposition:

> Honour your partners.
> Honour your corners.
> Now all join hand and circle left –
> Left around the ring.
> Circle back in the same old track
> And everybody swing.

Within a week or two the dancers had progressed to the do-si-do, and to
even more complicated routines. Albert became an ever more competent
caller. He had been studying David Miller's square dancing lessons in the
Daily Herald. Even Meirion acknowledged his competence, though he
might have been less effusive if he had known of its source, he never
having sullied his hands with that 'Socialist rag'. Indeed, Albert became
so skilled that he was soon improvising after the manner of the best of
the American callers:

> Come on, Shirley, don't you cheat,
> Rush old Meirion off his feet!

He could even rise to the trickier rhythms:

> If you ever want your minister to jump and jive,
> Marry him off to a dancing wife.

And one night, in a moment of unaccustomed religious inspiration, he let
rip with:

Give your testimonies, one an' all –
One more beat and the Lord may call.

Every Thursday evening Mrs Rachel Morris supervised the refreshments. She did not dance, but entered into the spirit of the occasion to the extent of wearing a hat decorated with the Stars and Stripes. Her grandson had bought it at Blackpool, and she had obliterated the words, 'Kiss me quick' with a sensitively placed sprig of heather (not that anyone would have taken the risk). American style hot dogs being unheard of in those parts, she had no difficulty clearing the plates of drop scones and fairy cakes. During the break for refreshments her daughter Shirley sang a solo. This was an opportunity she could not resist, despite having been whirled around by Meirion for the previous hour. That did little to aid her top notes, but nobody seemed to notice either that or the stylistic disparity between 'The Virginia Reel' and 'Seated one day at the organ ...'

As they stood by the tea urn on the first evening Betty Pugh and Dilys Jones were in earnest conversation.

'Where on earth did Elwyn get those clothes?'

'They didn't come from Newbridge Co-op, that's for sure.'

As they were speaking Elwyn himself came up and caught their general drift.

'Smashing, aren't they?' he beamed 'My older brother Emyr got them for me and sent them over.'

And Betty and Dilys remembered that Emyr had emigrated a few years before, and had become something in the music business in Nashville, Tennessee, where, they supposed, there were at least as many of those sort of clothes shops as Cardiff had Burtons.

Every Thursday evening Elwyn Roberts excused the senior children from homework so that they could join in the fun (and see him in his Western get-up). Every Thursday evening Jenkin and Dilys Jones arrived late, ostensibly because of the milking, but actually because after a long day Jenkin could take only so much of flinging a leg. Every Thursday evening Dai Cashbox (who else?) sat at the receipt of custom. He still did not know if the new Mrs Morgan could bake, but the dancing was doing very nicely. Of course, if she could bake as well that would be what Meirion would call an uncovenanted mercy, and what Dai knew as a bonus. And at the end of every Thursday evening the Reverend Elijah Morgan, having set a lively example to his flock, mopped his brow, mounted the platform, beamed upon the perspiring saints of Bethel, and offered the closing prayer.

www.ingramcontent.com/pod-product-compliance
Lightning Source LLC
Chambersburg PA
CBHW051837020726
47502CB00005B/1824